COLLISION

MERLE KRÖGER

TRANSLATED FROM THE GERMAN BY
RACHEL HILDEBRANDT AND ALEXANDRA ROESCH

The Unnamed Press
Los Angeles, CA

The Unnamed Press
P.O. Box 411272
Los Angeles, CA 90041

Published in North America by The Unnamed Press.

ISBN: 978-1-944700-19-5

Originally published in German as Havarie by Merle Kröger,
© 2015 Argument Verlag. All rights reserved.

Translation © 2017 Rachel Hildebrandt and Alexandra Roesch.

Cover image is a still from the film "Havarie"
a pong film production
directed by Philip Scheffner
written by Merle Kröger and Philip Scheffner
93 min., Germany 2016
(www.havarie.pong-berlin.de)

1 3 5 7 9 10 8 6 4 2

Library of Congress Control Number: Available Upon Request

This book is distributed by Publishers Group West

Cover design & typeset by Jaya Nicely

The translation of this work was supported by a grant from
the Goethe-Institut. The Goethe-Institut strengthens the dialogue
and cooperation of international literary relations and
contributes to disseminating German literature abroad.

FOR SISI

COLLISION

THE NIGHT BEFORE

Lalita Masarangi and Joseph Quezón

At ang iyong mata'y bilang lumuha
Ng di mo napapasin
Pagsisisi at sa isip mo't nalaman
Mong ika'y nagkamali
Nagsisisi at sa isip mo'y
Nalaman mong ika'y nagkamali...

The Dolphins at Dawn are wrapping up their last song on the stage over the swimming pool. The audience has drifted away. No, wait. There's the girl in the floral pantsuit crouched next to the plastic palm tree—been staring into the mirror app of her iPhone for hours now, her hunched body a concentrated failure. Her girlfriends are gone, giggling behind some door to the inside cabins. And the boy she was seen with earlier on Deck 5? When everything was still glittering? Also gone.

White swaths of steam float across the deck. It reeks. Someone has puked into the swimming pool, and fibrous chunks float on the surface. Leg of duck in a truffle reduction—the chef's daily special. As though in slow motion, the girl straightens up, staggers away, reeling between stacks of deck chairs and disappearing into the haze.

Lalita is very, very close to the edge of the pool and hums along as Jo croons in Tagalog. She's googled the language of the Philippines out of boredom, and also, she can't stop thinking about this Asian boy with the dreadlocks. He sings with his own voice now, eyes closed. No feigned American accent. No second, third, or fourth skin. Lalita sways. Or is it the boat swaying? It's the damned high heels, twelve centimeters of steel dressed in velvet. Doesn't matter, she's off the clock. Lalita Masarangi: *Spirit of Europe* security team, on duty from eight A.M. to eight P.M., seven days a week, with two half-hour breaks a day, plus overtime—three months on, one month off. Fucking nightmare. On day nineteen today. "Fulfill your dream in the western Mediterranean."

Open your eyes, Jo—look at me!

Jo opens his eyes, and the house amid the rice fields north of Manila fades like the afterimage of a dream. One last glance at Grandma Bella, who is using her stick to straighten up, her eyes gleaming out of the wrinkled face, transfixing him. Joseph, with his Afro, is proof of her love for the American she met in the forest of Mount Arayat, as they fled the Japanese fascists.

Now there's Gurkha Girl (that's what he secretly calls her) dressed to the nines. She looks so cool in her work uniform—black slacks, green beret, guerilla style—but the glittering miniskirt and the heels she's wearing tonight are cheap. Gurkha Girl turned Nepalese slut. With her eye shadow too blue, her curls too fake, the cool danger is gone. There's something else instead, a possibility that turns him on. Her eyes are closed; she's swaying with the rhythm as Jo turns away and Raymond on bass smiles and nods. Your night, Jo. Jo without an *e*.

Break free just once.

The playlist from Gold Cruises' company headquarters in Miami is two hours of G-rated pop music, strictly UK and

US charts. Two hours of the most boring shit in the world, regurgitated three times a day.

You might look like Jimi Hendrix, but the old biddies want Bob Marley at most, got it?

No woman, no cry.

Midday in the Maharaja Lounge, afternoons in the Star Lounge, evenings on the promenade deck or poolside, depending on the announcement. Seven days a week for ten weeks, three weeks off. Today is the eighth day of their third trip. Today Jo gazed into Gurkha Girl's eyes and whispered into the microphone, "'Anak,'" feeling the glares of the other band members on his back. The song could cost them their contract, but Jo knows they won't be able to resist playing it.

Break free just once.

Be ourselves just once.

The band repeats the chorus of the Filipino megahit a final time. Then silence. Rustling. The wind grows louder.

Hey.

Much louder than before.

Gurkha Girl stumbles and smiles.

EAST OF GHAZAOUET | ALGERIA

Karim Yacine

On the edge of the bluff, Karim watches the dark sea. The tingling is back, about two centimeters below his left shoulder blade. Since his bout with shingles, it's a recurring itch. Bad omen? Oh, come on, old man, it's just a signal from your body: it wants to be off again, wants to smell rubber and salt water; the rush of blood in your veins, dolphins hunting alongside the boat. This is how it feels to be alive!

Algeria is stagnation, death.

A sharp gust yanks him back to reality. The fire down on the beach blazes much too brightly as the men pack up their things in its glow. They are restless: the Harragas, *les brûleurs*, the passport burners. One of them looks up, pointing to where the boat is camouflaged. They are waiting on his signal to cast off, and Karim raises his hand to calm them. He is the oldest. Allah, how time flies. This will be his sixth trip—nobody has done this more times.

If the wind dies down in the next ten minutes, Karim decides, they will take off. If not, then they will spend another night pretending to be harmless dudes on a camping trip— young guys wasting their lives because they have no future anyway. Not here at least. They are the children of the Black Decade.

Black as this night.

The wind abates, Karim tugs the pull cord, and the outboard roars to life, brutally loud, echoing back from the craggy mountain walls. Let's get the hell out of here. He steers the boat so that the mountain is at his back. Like a shadow, they slide from the darkness. Karim knows it—no need to turn around because he feels the mountain there, its mass and magnitude.

He can also sense the invisible mountain rising from the bottom of the sea and partitioning the water halfway between Africa and Europe, just like in the Koran, verse 53 of Surah Al-Furqan 25. According to legend, Jacques Cousteau discovered this underwater watershed and then converted to Islam. In the films, the men on board the *Calypso* float over a secret universe. Karim has seen all the shows and docs, rerun on Algerian television, but *World without Sun* is his favorite, perhaps because the title fits his own world so perfectly.

He feels the extinct volcano northeast of Almería before he even activates the GPS. A swell of tapered boulders point like fingers toward the sea, showing him the way to the bay, where he will end up right in the middle of Cabo de Gata–Níjar Natural Park. In just fourteen hours, they'll have passed these three mountains, if all goes well. *Inshallah.*

The moon briefly lights up their faces, before vanishing completely behind a cloud: two distant cousins from Oran at the bow, ones he had not seen since they were children; next to them, the teacher from Algiers; Abdelmjid from the shop in Ghazaouet, where his mother buys her dates; two boys from his neighborhood, whose brothers long ago went to France. Karim had gone to school with them, and damn it—why in the world is he actually still here?

The other five from the village at the end of the bay had been forced on him by the guy who had sold him the rubber raft. Three boats for the price of two is what he offered, but Karim won't be part of this new scam for multiple takeoffs.

Three depart, only one makes it. The unlucky ones drown before the eyes of the coast guard. Algerian roulette.

You're getting old, Karim Yacine. Thirty-eight this fall. Old and anxious—Zohra was the first to notice it. He Skypes with her every day, assuming the internet is working.

"Don't be so impatient, Karim. Don't worry, we'll find a way."

He fears never again burying his face in her hair before he dies; it's this fear driving him across the sea.

"Promise me you'll never do it again!" Her face pixelates with anger over Skype, but regardless she is afraid, too, and he can see that. He promises. He breaks his promise. Not an encouraging start to a marriage. I promise you, Zohra, this is the last time—the journey and the lies. Without this, there is no future for us at all.

White gulls emerge soundlessly from the darkness and circle the boat. Karim follows them with his eyes, half hypnotized by their ghostlike forms. They fly up again and again, making 180-degree turns and then swooping down toward the frothy water that his motor leaves behind in the wave troughs. There comes another one, its feathers flaring up against the black sea—a white gleam brushed within a few seconds by a finger of light.

"Watch out, coast guard!"

Karim swings the rudder around hard, as shots ring out across the water. "Don't be afraid! They're just warning shots!" he calls out to his people. The cousin at the bow suddenly disappears, plunging into the darkness. Panic.

"Brother! Where are you?"

The spotlight sends a beam of light into the darkness, flickering as it searches across the sky.

"We've got to get away from here!"

"No!" Despair echoing through the night.

The roar of a motor, fingers of light. They are very close.

"Up there!" Abdelmjid's face is right next to his own. Karim leans to the left, looking past Abdelmjid. A wall. Their escape is located behind a bank of fog, so he steers blindly toward it. And then they are already plunging into it, the howling of the wind dying a swift death as the edge of the fog turns into a three-dimensional field of whitish light spreading outward, yearning for infinity, lapping at the edges of their small boat.

Karim kills the motor. Nobody says a word. All are thinking the same thing: If he's lucky, they'll pull him out of the water in time. If not...

The other cousin has buried his face in his hands, grieving silently until the fog swallows him.

ORAN HARBOR | ALGERIA

Oleksij Lewtschenko

Along the coastal road atop the cliffs of Oran, the illuminated high-rises tower into the night. The fog amplifies the light many times over and casts it back across the harbor and the Bassin d'Arzew like a floodlight.

Arzew or Arzeu (Berber: Erziouw) is the transshipment port for gas and oil from the Sahara, forty-two nautical miles northeast of Oran (Arabic: Wahrān), itself a container and ferry port and the second-largest city in Algeria with 678,000 residents.

The Plague, by Albert Camus, a French novel from the series Classics from the Twentieth Century (Folio Press, Kharkiv), was set here. When had he read that? Sometime back in the nineties?

A summer evening, but the fog has chilled him, Oleksij Lewtschenko. Oleksij from Oleksa, Greek origin: Alexander. Lewtschenko: son of Lewko. Lewtschenko, like Anatoli Lewtschenko, the Soviet cosmonaut of Ukrainian heritage. Back in December '87, Anatoli had third position in the Sojus TM-4 mission to the MIR Space Station. A single week in space and then immediately back to Earth to be a Soviet hero, awarded the Order of Lenin, and dead less than a year later of a brain tumor. What happened to you up there, Anatoli, my friend? What did you see?

Olek Lewtschenko: but to everyone on the *Siobhan* he's just "Chief." Chief engineer and master of the heart of the freighter, powered by nine MAK engine blocks manufactured in Kiel, Germany (though MAK is now actually a subsidiary of Caterpillar). Bloody globalization, our life and our ruin. It's the truth, though, isn't it? Give us the carrot and the stick—at least that's the case for us here at sea.

Standing on Deck A at the end of the gangway, Olek peers at the city through the fog. He squints, convinced that when you squint your eyes you can imagine that you are in Marseille and not in Oran—works even better after a few vodkas. Dmitri doesn't agree at all. A harbor, he says, thrives because of its bars and its women. By this standard, Oran is a dead fish. "The atmosphere, Olek. That's what matters!"

He watches the Algerian workers on the pier as they demount the hoses through which the oil has been pumped into the veins of his insatiable *Siobhan*.

"Olek, here it goes!" That's Dmitri, or rather, the captain.

In the haze, you can hardly see your own hands. Olek curses and tries to count the people from customs who are materializing out of the fog and approaching the *Siobhan*. Son of a bitch.

"If I can't see anything, you really can't," he mumbles up toward the bridge. A fraction of a second later, his walkie-talkie crackles.

"Olek!"

Of course.

"How many today, Olek?" it squeaks, and Olek can recite the words of this conversation, he's heard them so often. He and Dmitri are like an old married couple. They have been crossing the seas on the *Siobhan* for six years now, kept together after a fashion by Collins, the Irish shipowner.

He and Dmitri: the senior citizens out here—no doubt back home in Odessa they'd be cruising the Itaka club's Over

Forty Night. The Filipinos travel until they get married, then they use their pay to build a cute little cottage on the beach and settle down. And the officers are getting younger and younger, fresh out of the academy in Odessa, St. Petersburg, or wherever else.

Shrill beeping distracts him from counting anymore. The *Siobhan*'s two deck cranes are hefting containers into its open gullet, as the second officer hurries around, supervising the loading. Up and down between the containers is not without its dangers, but it's the only sport you can pursue here on board. And the stairs, obviously, a zillion times a day. On the large tankers, the crew members can bike and jog on deck, but not here. Every last centimeter is taken up by the containers. You can scoot by to the left or right only if your stomach is flat enough.

Man, how much still needs to be loaded? Will we ever cast off? He always thinks that, but at some point, it's over, often in the middle of the night, and finally comes the moment for Dmitri's favorite request: "Would the chief engineer be so kind as to start the engines?"

Chief's glory always arrives.

They are transporting empties again today. Full containers to Africa and empties back to Europe, as Algeria continues to consume, its exports at zero except for oil and gas—that's what they live from here.

Algeria (Arabic: al-Jazā'ir), officially the People's Democratic Republic of Algeria, is the largest country on the African continent. The majority of the population lives in northern Algeria, which is also where the Tell Atlas is located. The larger southern region is virtually uninhabited, dominated as it is by the desert regions of the Sahara. Gas, though, lies under the sand.

At least they aren't slaughtering each other right now. Algiers and Oran are the last North African harbors open to intra-Mediterranean hauling operations. Tunis, Casablanca, Tangiers—the big ships go there. Libya is sinking into chaos, Syria into war. Last year, in Beirut, an unexploded rocket landed in the *Siobhan*'s cargo hold. So close—they escaped a major catastrophe only by the skin of their teeth.

And Europe? The other side. The 2008 crisis, then the domino effect straight across the Continent. In principle, he has always preferred to stay close to Russia—a mistake as it's turned out now, but Olek wonders if he really wants to be a future EU citizen.

The Algerians are all there. "Eight," he mutters into the radio.

Actually, it might be nine coming up the gangway right now, or seven. Dmitri is worried that they will pick up another stowaway. You never can tell in North Africa: they will venture on board dressed up as customs officers while the actual ones stay back on land and quietly count their money. And then, when you are on the high sea, suddenly someone pops up in front of you, someone you have never seen before. "Europe," he will proclaim. Then Dmitri has to call up the shipowner. And he is the one who calculates what it will cost to ditch the stowaway—that is, if you can find a European harbor that'll let you drop him there.

"*Salaam alaikum,*" the Algerians murmur, pushing past him.

"It's nine, Olek, nine," the device on his belt barks. "Can't you count, or are you drunk?"

Olek nods. Nine after all.

"Don't just blow this off, bro. Collins doesn't give a fuck. In less than three days, we'll be sitting on a plane back home. And then what, Olek? What would we do?"

Olek nods. You're right, Captain Dmitri.

The great captain. Always in uniform, always proper. The officers idolize him. Ersatz father for the Filipinos on the crew. A man you can look up to. Dmitri does not care that he has the oldest tub in Collins's fleet under his command. Bottom line, he's the captain.

No matter how stressful it is these days, seafaring remains his passion. In each harbor he goes ashore if they are anchored long enough: coffee with the charterers, gifts for the crew. Yesterday, he brought back a verse from the Koran framed in gold for the crew's mess, which also serves as a conference room. All welcome here on board, so Koran for Arabic visitors and the framed Madonna for the Filipinos. Something for everyone, just like with the food. Through a crewing agency in Cyprus, Dmitri scrounged up a cook who can literally do it all: halal, kosher, Asian. He can cook you around the world, if you want him to. Makes better borscht than Olek's mother.

"Go ashore!" Dmitri's missionary zeal truly grates the nerves sometimes. "Live a little, Chief!"

Live a little. Olek wishes he had the time. They have to be in Cartagena by early tomorrow morning. Time is money! Collins's money, of course, not theirs. If Olek wants a distraction, he finds it on Wikipedia and VesselFinder Pro.

Engine noise pierces the fog. Not bad—sounds like it has a little more horsepower than us. Curious, Olek steps onto the gangway, opening the photo app on his cell phone. Always prepared.

Behind the *Siobhan*, the coast guard comes into view, steaming full speed toward the pier before being secured. The phone disappears into his pocket. The Algerian authorities do not joke around when it comes to taking photos of their harbor area. National security. Olek watches as a damp bundle is tossed ashore.

Shit. Nothing left to do for that one.

He crosses himself.

A body.

Not a good night.

SPIRIT OF EUROPE | BRIDGE

Léon Moret

"*Titanic* alarm!" His deep voice is a big asset, and he knows it. First officer of the third-largest cruise ship in the world at the age of twenty-six! It helps that he sounds older, no doubt about it. And thanks to a directive from Miami, leadership seminars are offered on board, mandatory for everyone with direct reports. You get classified as an analyzer or harmonizer, showrunner or neophyte—a bunch of types. Léon is an analyzer. Analyzes the facts first and then acts.

On duty, the second in command is already on his way to the searchlights. A silent shadow in front of the panorama window of the bridge, his strides are swallowed into the thick blue carpet. Everything is blue up here. The bridge is Léon's *lieu de prédilection*, his playground. If you were to ask him where he wanted to die, he would answer without hesitation: "Up here."

Such thoughts come to you on the bridge, alone in the dark, eyes burning from staring out at the black sea for hours on end, as five thousand people sleep beneath you. On this trip, precisely 3,778 passengers and 1,259 crew members—the fate of all in a twenty-six-year-old's hands. It's like being high, dude. You can feel the power with every fiber of your body. Jedi-like, big time. Night duty between twelve and four. Seven days a week.

The day shift is boring by comparison; they usually just lie in the harbor, except for sea days like tomorrow. Crisscrossing the Mediterranean, so the guests can lie in the sun and we can pass the time until Palma de Mallorca. Ten weeks of duty, then ten weeks off. When Léon has time off, he moves in with Mado on Deck 1.

His wife has a different contract; she has to stay on board longer. She is the guest reception manager and works front of house every day from morning to night. That would really freak him out. So much more responsibility than up here. But that's Mado, a social genius. In order to be together, they cruise and work in rotation, their life taking place on the *Europe*. It's not that bad, really. A small city in which people from more than fifty nations live together peacefully and party every evening. Which home around the world can match that? Exactly—none.

Léon blinks a couple of times. The couple outside dance in the light of their mobile phones near the prow of the ship, and he cannot gaze directly at their flashlight apps for very long, the bright light intensified by the fog. The quartermaster, a Croat, has retreated to the stern with his binoculars. The girl in the glittering miniskirt seems vaguely familiar to Léon. She stretches out her arms, the boy standing very close behind her. Her long hair is teased by the wind as they get ready for the selfie. One, two—

At that moment, Kiyan, his second in command, switches on the searchlight. The couple stumbles backward, shocked, and Léon laughs out loud. Kiyan gently guides them back to the side deck with his spotlight. Léon relaxes. When the darkness is disrupted for too long, his eyes take ages to readjust. That's the way it is here. Everything's done by hand. No shortcuts. The captain of the *Spirit of Europe* is old school; he used to steer boats with a wheel and not with a joystick. Though now he doesn't show up much on the bridge, since he's constantly stuck in the office on conference calls with Miami. His motto: If you only rely on your instruments, then go into aviation. That is why it's pitch black here. A couple of control lamps flicker, their light subdued. Kiyan's monitors are behind the curtain, logbook and radar. Léon and the quartermaster keep the warning lights on only for emergencies, even in the restrooms.

"They're gone now," Kiyan mumbles in his quiet voice.

"Go fuck your brains out," Leon adds.

The Croat laughs, a tad too loudly for Léon's taste. Suddenly he snatches up the binoculars. "Damn, something up ahead!"

Léon feels the adrenaline rush and jumps up. They are still stuck in the fog bank, damn it. It's been soup since Gibraltar. Yellow condition. Visibility less than a hundred meters. "Kiyan, call the old man."

Kiyan is already dialing. Léon jogs over to the stern, mostly because he needs the exercise. The Croat—what is his name again?—points toward the water. "It was there a minute ago." Now the wall has closed again, *tutto completto.*

Léon sprints back and switches on the Elephant's Ear, which they use to listen to the soundscape. The roar of the wind and sea slams into his eardrum. There is something out there, no doubt. Machines.

"Kiyan?"

Kiyan comes toward him, thumbs-up. The captain has given his authorization, and Léon pushes the button.

The foghorn sounds.

The noise spreads like a mushroom cloud, powerful and all-encompassing. Léon throttles the speed and stares back into the night. If only the five thousand passengers below him knew how damned full this ocean is, how many near accidents there are. It's a fucking interstate out here.

A dark shadow interrupts his line of sight, off the stern. The freighter is cutting across their path. They must have seen them; at night, the *Europe* is lit up like a Christmas tree.

"*Siobhan*, Ireland," he hears Kiyan's voice. "Freighter. Should we radio them?"

What's the use? Léon stands up against the panorama window. They are in a damned hurry, fifteen men, at most, on a rusty old barge filled to the brim with containers. He should feel sorry for them, the poor buggers.

Léon changes course, and the mighty ship bows to his will, though not without bucking slightly.

What do you want from me, little man?

Yet Léon knows: the force is with him.

Marwan Fakhouri

A load of dirty sheets comes tumbling out of the chute and lands on the floor because he forgot to push the trolley underneath it again. Marwan feels the panic rise up in him. Always from bottom to top, up from his stomach, then a tightness in his neck and hyperventilation. He knows the symptoms. No mirror necessary to watch himself turn pale as his hands begin to shake. This noise is terrible down here. And the heat! Sweat runs down his forehead; he wipes his sleeve across his eyes. An all too familiar gesture. Nothing used to affect him. Double shift in the operating theater, short nap, then back on. No shaking, never.

The girl from China wordlessly pulls up the laundry container and starts collecting the wash. Her face is expressionless, her body narrow and sinewy. She could be seventeen or thirty.

Working side by side with him every night for almost a month, she has never spoken to him—not a single word. The Chinese laundry crew changes every few weeks. Most are men, with a few occasional women. In the beginning, Marwan tried his best to start a conversation—tried in English—but the reaction was always the same: a smile, a shake of the head. Anyhow, it is so loud down here. There is always a machine spinning somewhere, you can barely understand yourself.

The Chinese come and go. Marwan and Oke stay.

Obviously, we have only ourselves to blame. We are the damned on this death boat, the long dead. We don't need anything: No daylight in the laundry or daylight in the cabin. No daylight in the crew canteen. A clandestine cigarette outside, in front of the crew-only gym, and a quick glance at the sky—ideal holiday weather. But not for us. The dead don't need holidays.

The boat rolls beneath him, and Marwan's stomach protests. The seasickness hadn't developed until he'd been on the ship a few weeks. He'd felt good at first, relieved to have escaped the rubber raft, to be in a safe place for once. Practically euphoric. Then the dizziness set in, and he began to walk as if on eggshells, with this feeling of never being quite right. And the constant nausea. He eats but can't keep it down. He eats. He forces himself to eat.

Machine fourteen at the far back, one of the big drums for sheets, stops. And then the next sound, unbearable, penetrating: this digital whistle. Marwan drags himself over and opens the drum and the whistling stops. He backs away as hot steam billows out. Reaching for an empty trolley with his right hand, his left begins to yank the clammy, tangled sheets out of the machine.

If only they could at least work together, he and Oke, the boy from Lagos, but their cabin is tiny, and they have only one bunk bed. The stale air is just about enough for one. One works, while the other one sleeps.

The sheets cling to one another. Marwan's sore hands are simply too weak.

Surgeon's hands. Mother had stared at his hands for countless minutes, the day he was accepted to medical school. My son, a surgeon. Pride of the nation. Ha! Nothing left of that now. He cannot suppress the shaking even when he concentrates. Marwan operates only while lying sleepless on his bunk, regardless of whether it is day or night outside. The narrow cabin is always stale with perspiration, cheap air-conditioning, and chemical cleaning fluids, as he fights against forgetting, stitches a wound, amputates a leg. But the images are increasingly blurred.

Exhausted, he lets go of the tangled mass of damp cotton. Another attempt.

"Leave it!" Did she just speak to him?

Did she?

She pushes him aside and detangles the sheet with three quick shakes. "Do this! It's easier." She points toward the rotary iron. Marwan looks around.

All the others quietly slave away. One or the other wipes off the sweat. He feels like he is hallucinating. She again indicates the rotary iron. Marwan smiles. When did he last smile? He can no longer remember. It feels strange as the corners of his mouth lift. She does not smile, just turns away and goes back to the chute to fetch more fodder for the insatiable, monstrous washing drums. Marwan slumps against the wall, just for a moment.

There are slips of paper hanging across from him, like everywhere else down here in the labyrinthine entrails of the ship. Next Monday is payday. Ten till six, every two weeks. Last time he fell asleep in the line. He did not even wake up when they finally called his name. Jordan Baker. Security had kept his passport, and somehow along the way Marwan had turned into Jordan Baker in the personnel department's computer. American citizen with a valid Social Security number. Oke is also called Jordan Baker. They share the name, so to speak. Nobody cares what your name is here anyway. Night shift laundry duty. A no-name.

Next to the week's payroll announcement, a leaflet for the onboard money transfer service to all countries in the world. The exchange rate is worse than Western Union's, but he and

Oke have no choice. They cannot go on land in the next harbor, so they send money home every two weeks. Now and then, very rarely, an email.

"Sorry, dear Mother, that I haven't written for so long. I finally found work on a ship. I haven't had any time yet to find myself a place to live in Spain. I am a junior doctor for night shifts, Mother, I have to start right from the bottom again, but what can I do?"

His mother's answers are long, always revolving around the same topic. She complains of tiredness. Otherwise, there is nothing to report of life on the Syrian Mediterranean coast. Waiting for Father to come home from work. Waiting for the war to end. Waiting for her son to come home. Waiting for grandchildren. Waiting.

Oke has started lying. He claims this is what his family wants. Nobody back home in Nigeria is interested in stories about failure. Failure is a private thing, Oke reasons, and laughs. Each week, he writes elaborate stories about his life on the luxury ship where he started out as a temporary waiter before becoming a barkeeper, and now, just three months later, he is already dining room manager.

Enough musing. You can never be sure—the Indian has installed his cameras everywhere. A creepy guy, never sleeps, always stalking through the corridors with that quiet, bouncing stride, nothing but empty promises in his pockets: *Maybe next week. We are negotiating. Miami is negotiating. Nobody wants you.* Who knows what he would do if I stopped doing my job properly.

Marwan gently pushes off the wall and takes three steps. He removes a sheet from the basket and slowly feeds it into the roller. If he makes a mistake, the rotary iron will stop working. Slowly, centimeter by centimeter, the cotton disappears between the rollers. The smell reminds him of his childhood. The laundry in the yard right behind the house. A pipe coming out of the wall, white steam, day and night. Sun on the red stone. His cat.

He waits for a moment, then picks up the sheet again at the bottom. It is smooth and fresh, like new. He wishes he could restart his life like that, too. A new beginning.

Suddenly, the ship lurches, the dizziness starts up, and Marwan drops the sheet, staggering sideways and reaching into nothing as he smashes his head against the frame of the clothes rail that is bolted down, like everything else on this boat.

The Chinese woman turns around immediately, alarmed, on watch—as if she had anticipated that something like this would happen. Everyone else carries on with their work.

Darkness.

Lalita Masarangi and Joseph Quezón

Entertainers' cabins have portholes. Even if it's totally foggy out there, the claustrophobia isn't as fierce. And no bunk beds. So this is what it feels like to lose your virginity in an entertainer's cabin.

"Gurkha Girl!" His voice is raw and demanding. Lalita, motionless, likes this name, which he whispers as his mouth travels over her body, closely followed by shudders that brush across her skin like a light breeze.

Gurkha Girl. Her male ancestors were twelve generations of Gurkhas, proud elite soldiers in service to the English Crown. Proud idiots who strutted about like peacocks in front of the Queen, who let themselves be slaughtered under the symbol of the crossed daggers. And when they didn't die, which didn't happen very often, they obediently went back to where they came from after finishing their work. How fucking stupid.

Not that Lalita thinks her ancestors were ridiculous.

On the contrary. Only four years ago, she had desperately wanted to be one of them. If only this beautiful boy from the islands knew how right he was. Gurkha Girl, that's me. Lalita Masarangi from Gurkha Town, Aldershot, UK.

Ah, so this is what it feels like. Carry on, Island Boy.

Wherever his mouth goes, Jo feels the slight shuddering of her body beneath his. Suddenly it hits him, the realization that this body is young. Younger than his, full of pulsing blood, with muscles whose strength he can feel and skin soft as foam, which turns to nothing when you cup it in your hand. Jo wants to have this body, wants to own it. He grasps her leg, pushing it outward, violently. He wants to—he has to be inside her. "Come on, bitch!" Deeper. Take me in.

But it's too late. The wave comes from behind this time. It is high, higher than in the nightmares from his childhood.

His mother, far away in Kuala Lumpur, is taking care of a stranger's children when it starts. Grandmother Bella is old already, but her anger burns fierce. And she gets very angry when he calls for his mother in his sleep. She invents stories about a wave, higher than her house, which will swallow him if he doesn't stop crying.

Much later, when he sees the images of the tsunami, he knows that Bella did not lie. And that she can summon a tsunami—or put another way, it's probably best to ask what old Bella Quezón cannot do. She even went to court and now gets a pension from the government, because she fought for the liberation. By the way, Jo's mother never came back. She married her employer. A practical solution, since from then on he didn't even have to pay her to watch his kids. She still sends money to Bella and Jo, each year at Christmas.

The wave comes and smashes him against Gurkha Girl's body, whose muscles immediately turn to steel. He hears her pant, gasping for breath. He already feels the water, salty on his face.

"Jo?" Lalita doesn't understand. What's going on? Did she do something wrong? "Did I—?" He shakes his head and buries his face between her breasts.

Gasping rapidly, she feels dizzy. Something is burning inside, deep inside. Am I not a virgin anymore, or what? Oh man, twenty-three and so bloody stupid!

While the white trash chicks in Aldershot were having endless sex, Lalita had just one goal: In ten years, I'll be dead!

Dead, because she would be killed in action for the British Crown. Or suicide, because she'd messed up the entrance examination. So Kathmandu. Wake up at five every morning. Train, train, train. Like a mantra, she longed for death, tortured herself for death. Death seemed so much brighter, so much more intense, so much more dramatic than life. Was that really a surprise? She lost the first love of her life when he fell in love with her brother and they ran off together to London. All of Aldershot shot its mouth off then, because the son of a former elite soldier was, well, basically gay.

Dead or suicide. Fuck it. And now I'm lying here with this boy, who is beautiful enough to die for, ready to die. All for nothing again.

Jo can't talk about it. He can't tell Gurkha Girl that he's been fucking rich women for weeks to earn extra cash, that he can't stand himself. But that's the way it is. The ship's pay is a joke. You can't even get an apartment in a Manila slum for that. Raymond does perfume sales during the day, the drummer does the sound engineering for the other bands on the boat, and the pianist also plays for the ice show. Jo started with a part-time job in the casino, the last three hours on the blackjack table. The guy who was on before him, an American, wanted to give him half his shift. "Got something better to do." Wink. And then: "Don't miss out, mate!" Another wink. High five. Two hours later, Jo knew what he meant.

The black-haired chain-smoker on crutches, with diamonds in her ears and wads of dollars—she lost and smoked, lost and smoked, lost. Her voice was hoarse from the endless cigarettes, and she swore quietly to herself in a language he didn't understand. Eyes hard as pebbles. At the end, there was a roll of dollar bills in front of him on the table. She was the first.

"I need some air!" Jo has to get away. He doesn't want to fall in love with this girl. He wants to scrape money together, lots of money, and then finally record his album. His own songs are his only chance. He has to get out of here now.

"Stay as long as you want. So sorry." And he's out the door, without a single backward glance.

Barely an hour later, his body slices through the waves. Jo doesn't die straightaway. He fights his way back up to the surface and sees the ship, full of lights, full of life, slowly growing smaller. Sees the first shimmer of dawn. And turns himself, quite calmly now, toward the wave that engulfs him.

Havarie (Collision)
Position: 37°20′N 0°49′W
Radius: 12 nautical miles
Begins: 1:53 P.M. CET

SPIRIT OF EUROPE | DECK 10

Léon Moret

Léon is asleep.

In his dream, he runs along Broadway, the ship's nerve tract. Broadway: What cynical joker came up with that one? With none of the pomp and circumstance of the upper decks, here it's all slogging and sweating. Supplies are heaved, trash is shunted, laundry is hauled along in sacks.

Léon's looking for Mado. Faces blurred. The global working class runs as if chased, reporting for duty just in the nick of time. Nobody, not even your best friend, smiles at you. Facial muscles are off duty. The whole phony display of friendship is off the table down here, with the fear of the cameras on your tail. Here you see stress, tension, bags under the eyes. The first wrinkles. Léon gives a smile here and there, nods to someone. He usually still has something left in the tank after his lonely nights on the bridge. He could run around naked in the dark up there and it wouldn't bother anyone. A streaking officer. Ha!

Léon walks and walks. Broadway never ends, on and on between the sickly yellow walls. Wasn't Mado here just a moment ago? The smell grows more revolting. As if someone were slowly turning up a dial. Trash, vomit, piss, mold.

Smile. Nod. You're an officer. Don't let on about anything. People rush past. Gloomy faces, man. Heat. Stench.

Smile, Léon. Mado! Is it her? He speeds up, breaks into a run. Sure is! It's Mado, in her uniform, her freshly sleeked hair forced into a perfect, round bun. Mado from the banlieues of Lyon. Here it doesn't matter where you come from. We're all equal. Léon from the Île d'Aix. Mado from Lyon. Léon is white; Mado, black.

We don't have a problem with it.

Léon's cabin is on Deck 10, Mado's on Deck 1, just above the waterline. Where Léon comes from, there are not even cars, just oysters, wind, and sea. Where Mado comes from, there're only the projects, and trash, and poisoned rivers—

A sharp jolt racks the boat.

Léon emerges from sleep like a drowning man. Shit, overslept. Darkness. This cabin is a curse and a blessing. No daylight. He has to sleep somehow.

The ship! What's going on?

The engines are never supposed to stop, under any circumstances. He listens to the faint drone. The machines run day and night, nonstop since the *Spirit of Europe* was in the dry docks four years ago. Power supply. Rudder. Even in the harbors.

What's happening? We're not moving anymore.

Léon jumps up, switching on his tablet. He reaches for the trousers hanging over the chair, inspects them: no stains on the crotch (the last hours up there were bloody boring). Boots up VesselFinder Pro. They're in the middle of the sea, twelve miles off Cartagena.

Button shirt. Léon blinks and stares at the small, colorful triangles, which have multiplied now that it's daytime. Worse every year. He clicks through the ship names. Some you meet time and again, like old friends. *Siobhan*, a cargo ship. The anarchist from last night, lying in Cartagena, as if butter wouldn't melt on its tongue. Carry on, nothing unusual. Shoes. Where are his fucking shoes? A glance in the mirror.

Léon, tired, disheveled. Léon, beach child. Green eyes. Green sea. Léon, child of the beach. Dinner in silence at the wooden table, with his father, Georges, grinding his jaw. Fanatical environmentalist. Geologist. He had developed a method for recycling old neon pipes into rare earth. The only sound is his older brother, Fabian, eating noisily.

Léon grimaces in front of the mirror. Smile, Léon.

Léon Moret. First officer.

Always on duty.

Countenance!

Lalita Masarangi

Quick, quick. She's switched on all four monitors, but the program takes forever to load. Come on. Lalita takes another drag on her joint. Stay calm now, come on, baby. She stubs out the joint and sticks the butt in her pocket before grabbing the air freshener. OMG! Why doesn't Nike get rose scent or something? Ocean breeze, of all things; everything stinks of ocean here anyway. What are we, fish? She feels the pot going to her head.

Footsteps outside the door.

It can't be Nike. He'll be on his inspection round for at least another thirty minutes. Suddenly she feels like the boat is slowing down. It can't be, must be the dope. There's no window in security headquarters. You don't need one— that's what the cameras are for. Lalita giggles. Wicked dope. Who knows what sort of stuff? She had taken the joint with her when she got up earlier. Her little revenge. How could Jo just disappear like that?

Jo, the bastard. She feels almost as shitty as when they turned her down in Nepal. Used. Lalita Masarangi, used Gurkha Girl, going cheap.

The program is finally up and running. Which camera first? Hey, approach it strategically. Camera on Deck 1, corridor starboard. She clicks through last night's recordings.

Here we go, there we both are. God, I look dreadful in that dress. Never mind. We've already gone past—

What's that? There's a guy coming out of his cabin. Wearing only his underpants and a potbelly. Yuck, gross. Disappears again.

Click.

Click.

It didn't feel that long, what we did inside—there he is. Jo, what on earth is the matter with you? You're running down the corridor as if a monster were after you. Jo. She presses pause, just before he passes the camera. *Tick. Tick. Tick.* Zooms in with the joystick. Jo is beautiful, even in pixelated black and white.

Click.

Click.

Lalita knows how to click from one camera to another in order to track someone. She grew up with it, sitting on Dad's lap. "Have a go, Princess." Daddy's girl.

Jo goes to the elevator. *Click.* Deck 3. No. Keep going. *Click. Click. Click.* Deck 4, 5, 6. Where's he going? Hectically she fiddles with the mouse, feels her heart pounding. Where are you going, Jo? What made you run away from me like that? Stop, back. Deck 5. Promenade deck and entrance to the casino. There he is. Casino. Black. Access denied.

"Access to the cameras in the casino requires a special code."

Oh.

No.

Nike.

She hadn't heard anything. Not a thing.

"For reasons of privacy." Piercing. Lalita jumps up, but he is beside her in three strides and leans over the table. His aftershave makes her feel sick. "Who are you spying on?"

Her thoughts race. Find an excuse. You have to make something up quick before your father ends up hearing about this.

Lalita doesn't look at Nike, as he takes the mouse out of her hand very gently. "Take a look, you little tramp." With three clicks he takes them back to the hallway image again. Jo and Lalita. God, I look like shit. "Are you crazy, girl?" he almost whispers, his hand at her chin, still very gentle, very gentle. "Take a look. Take a good look. He's sleeping off his trip somewhere, between two legs that are longer than yours."

Lalita gags as shame, mixing with bile, shoots into her mouth.

Swallow.

Nike's radio crackles. "Security chief to the bridge!"

She senses his impatience. He needs to bring this to an end. "We have an incident. I have to go up to the bridge, and you are to join your colleagues up on Deck 12 within the next five minutes. Patrol. Passengers are gathering starboard. A lot of them. Too many. Are you listening, girl? If just one of them gets the merest scratch, I will hold you personally responsible."

The door slams shut behind him.

Lalita doesn't move as the onboard loudspeaker crackles, Léon Moret's voice intoning: "Ladies and gentlemen, this is your first officer speaking. Some of you have probably noticed that we have stopped the engines. The reason is a stricken raft, alongside the vessel, starboard side. There is no cause for concern. The coast guard has..."

Lalita grabs her beret.

Deck 12.

Just a quick vomit first.

Seamus Clarke

Blue. Blue water, shot from above, no sky. Lightly rolling swell. The picture wobbles, while in the midst of the blue, a gray rubber raft dances on the waves. Many people are on it.

Too many.

Someone jostles his arm from the right, the side holding the camera. "Kelly lass, can you keep them away from me?" There's too much ruddy pushing and shoving up here.

"How many, Seamus? Tell me how many there are."

Oh, Kelly. I can't get a good count with all this shaking going on. Careful, zoom back out.

The raft with the people in it is growing smaller or the blue is growing bigger, depending on your point of view. A tiny boat in a massive expanse of blue. Another rough jolt sends the sky racing into view, the line between sea and horizon blurred by haze.

Seamus tries to focus in tight, but the boat keeps slipping out of the center of the frame. He zooms further out.

First, he can't make out the people anymore.

Then he can't make out the boat

All that remains is a black speck in the blue.

Seamus's focus gets lost. Where are we? His eye searches for something to catch on to, and his hand follows. Seamus pans to the right. Window fronts. The fitness studio. Then back to the left. People at the railing, silhouetted against the light. Downward: a crowd on Deck 4.

"Seamus!" Kelly tugs on his shirt. "Tell me, how many?!"

Lass, what do you want? I can't count them. Everything's shaking too much. Seamus lowers his camera for a moment.

Orientation: Where am I? Deck 12. A moment ago, everyone was sunning themselves on the loungers: Kelly, content with a Bloody Mary and her book, and Seamus, looking the other direction, with a view of the pool. The Upper Ten Thousand are enthroned straight across the way. Those with the suites are always nicely separated from the commoners, the ladies blinged out from head to toe. Today only the old woman with the wheelchair is there, without her companion. Hanging in the lounge chair like a wet rag, she looks a little lost and very alone. What is it they say? *It's not lonely at the top. There is a swimming pool.*

What was happening again? Oh, right, the belly flop contest. Men doing belly flops. The fatter you were, the better your chances of winning. Did you ever see a finer collection of chubby British specimens? Seamus had raised his glass and toasted the winner, then suddenly: "Ladies and gentlemen, this is your first officer speaking."

The bridge. Something had to be...

Seamus had snatched up his camera quicker than his mind could process the situation, and as he did, they came from behind, pressing him and his wee lady against the railing, as if they were handing out freebies up front.

People today have no respect. He glances around for her. Kelly shrugs, shoving a pushy crone aside before lying back down. "Just let me know when something exciting happens."

Seamus lifts the camera up to his eye. "Sure, lass, I won't leave my post." Even if he wanted to, he couldn't stop staring at the raft out there. Seamus stays put, which is almost second nature to him. Comes with the job.

Seamus is the night watchman at the Royal Victoria Hospital in Belfast. It is a giant box of sorts, its own borough, built out of bricks, with new glass and steel additions inserted here and there. Its specialty: gunshot wounds and brain injuries. Yes, that is the legacy of the Troubles, after almost forty years of civil war. There is a market niche for everything in this world.

Each evening, Seamus knots his tie and pets his Jack Russell terrier named Jack—yes, that is his name. Did I ever claim to be bloody James Joyce? He then walks out of his single-family bungalow at the end of the cul-de-sac in Dunmurry. All around are houses just like his, arranged in a crescent, like the set for a peaceful suburban neighborhood in a bloody BBC series. Seamus knows each of the men and women who emerge from these houses every day: average people who walk through their neatly manicured front yards on their way to their reliable cars.

South Belfast, Catholic through and through.

The war is over. Yes, it is, but people don't really change. They trust only their own. You don't buy a house to the east or the north of the city unless you are tired of being alive. And who wants to live among people who refuse to accept that the future is not on their side anyway? Who hold tightly to their British flags, which have not meant anything in a very long time? The future belongs to the Republic of Ireland, to Europe, to whatever. Do you see the guy over there coming out of the pub, in a jogging suit with a fag hanging out of his mouth? He used to be a bigwig in the IRA.

Every evening, Seamus drives toward the northern part of the city, through the rain. Dusk in Belfast lasts twice as long as anywhere else in the world. A battered armored police car cruises by. At least the gunfire has stopped. Just to be safe, Seamus prays a quick thank-you to the Virgin Mary for the fact that the Troubles are over. If you ask him (or one of his five brothers), he will tell you: No doubt about it, we don't belong to the hardliners. But don't get me wrong, the conflict was necessary—otherwise, those of us here would still be dancing to their pipes, like my wee Jack.

It's hard to imagine, but there were only farms and fields here after World War II. Our ancestors were housed down in the city, packed together like sardines in narrow, rented apartments. If you did not own property, you could not vote, so they made sure the Catholics could not own their own homes. It was as simple as that.

We Clarkes are a working-class family that finally got out of the slums and bought our own house in Turf Lodge in 1961. A new borough, Turf Lodge, ripped from the moors and lying in the shadow of Black Mountain. Lots of children, a wild herd. The street was our playground, steep enough for lethal soapbox races.

It was right over here, can't you see it? The city had not grown all the way out here back then. No buses drove this far out; there were no stores. We kids had to walk to school, an hour every day in all kinds of weather. That is one way to keep people down, but not us. We set up our own school, then the church, then the leisure center, then the social club.

Seamus waves at a woman with a permanent and a pink wool scarf, as she flits across the street with her umbrella. Nice old lady, right? She leads a funeral march every year, over at the graveyard. The British shot her son right here. And Mary, her oldest daughter, crazy girl, she lay up there on the roof holding a shotgun, loaded and cocked. She lives in Australia now. Mary, that is.

The windshield wipers are not making any headway against the rain. Seamus turns them up faster, and through the blurry glass, Kevin looks down at him from his mural. Hi, Kevin, my friend. You still wear your hair the way you did in the seventies. No one wears it like that anymore.

Kevin.

Get in.

From this point on, every day, Seamus always carries Kevin with him. He drives with Kevin to the Royal, toward the sea and past the other murals of the hunger strikers.

Good evening to you, too, Bobby Sands.

The Peace Wall divides the Catholic and the Protestant boroughs. Peace, well, you could call it that, I suppose. If you do not know your way around here, you will find yourself in point zero seconds stopped short in front of a wall topped with shards of glass. They recently started organizing bus trips for tourists: the Belfast Murals. After all, the entire city is full of them. We started it, then the loyalists copied us. Well, it is better than war.

Along with Seamus, Kevin gets out of the BMW, walks across the bridge from the parking deck to the clinic and through the warren of halls and corridors. Doors hum open automatically. Into the elevator. Ninth floor. One more hall. A windowless room full of monitors. His colleague leaves, cheerful now that his shift is over.

Seamus hangs up his jacket and sits down on the swivel chair. Come, Kevin, come here and take a look. Three hundred monitors, cameras everywhere in the Royal. People with head injuries often react erratically, are disoriented, grab at the clinic personnel. Seamus is supposed to anticipate such incidents—that is what he has been trained to do.

Don't you see, Kevin, if only I had known how to do this back then.

I could've prevented it.

I could've yelled out to you: "Piss off, mate, get a move on!"

I could've, right, Kevin?

Look, I can control every camera in this building; I can move them and zoom in on every corner. Do you recognize this, Kevin? Your room?

That is where you died, three days later, after the plastic bullet destroyed your brain.

Kevin, best friend. Seamus lowers his camera. He feels dizzy. Even today, this is what happens whenever he thinks about the day Kevin...

Oh well, never mind.

"What's wrong, luv?" Kelly pushes up her sunglasses and looks at him, concerned.

He shakes his head. "It's just so bloody hot."

And do they all have to keep screaming around him?

Perhaps he could go down to the Irish pub on the promenade and treat himself to an early pint. To be honest, he feels better down there than he does up here. It is dark and cool like at home. His Kelly and his brothers had pooled their money and given him this cruise for his fiftieth birthday, but Seamus misses Belfast, misses the rain.

Misses Kevin. Just like every other day for the past thirty-seven years.

He lifts the camera up one more time.

He has to look, has to see what is happening to the boys out there, has to pay attention. Kevin might be out there on that raft. Perhaps he is the one who keeps waving the red cloth around. Of course, that is complete and utter rot, but such ideas keep shooting through his mind. Who actually knows what is real?

Behind him, a British woman whines: "Why can't we keep going? Who really wants them? Their own people should come and fish them out."

Seamus presses the button. Recording.

He counts. "One, two, three—"

No, damn it. Can't she shut up?

Fucking Brits.

"One, two, three, four, five, six, seven..."

Marwan Fakhouri

The ship's engines are humming inside his head. He has swallowed the entirety of the huge ship, and now it is droning and stamping in rage. His head keeps expanding in order to accommodate the massive engines.

There, now. All in. Quiet outside his head, noise inside.

Marwan, concentrate.

"Fakhouri, diagnosis?" Is that the professor's voice?

Panic. Go on instinct.

"Brain hemorrhage?"

The exam, he wants to pass the exam.

"Precision, Fakhouri, precision."

"Arterial epidural hematoma."

The professor is standing opposite him in the operating room. In a moment, they will begin to open his skull. The bleeding must be stopped.

Halt. Stop.

Go back.

It can't be.

The professor had been hit by snipers, in his car on the way to the hospital in Aleppo. Blood everywhere; the bullet punctured his carotid artery. He bled to death at the traffic light. A coincidence, they said. Wrong place at the wrong time. Moments later came the Syrian army fighter jets and the bombing.

Another coincidence? They had treated the rebels. Rebels. Friends. Colleagues. Protesters. Patients. Kidnapped from the hospital by the security police.

Fast-forward: We operate day and night, in private homes, on dining room tables, alongside cupboards full of china, paintings on the walls.

Unbelievable.

We operate on provisional tables in mountain caves, with electricity from generators. At least until the lights go off. We will never let on where the secret clinics are. Never.

We do not trust anyone anymore.

"Where am I?"

Marwan sits up suddenly. The doctor, who is trying to take his blood pressure, jumps back, startled. His eyes dart around, trying to take in the room.

A hospital, all lit up. Bright fluorescents. Lighted cupboards. Instruments in sterile packaging. The woman is in green operating scrubs.

Marwan is terror-struck.

They got me.

Only Assad has hospitals like this, where the dissidents vanish. Forever.

I am lost.

Sybille Malinowski

He asks her to dance with him. It is already the third time this evening, and it has attracted attention. Thank goodness she came up with another way to jazz up that old outfit. No one will notice that it is the same one from last spring—the blouse with the buttons down the back and a bright sash at the waist. All eyes are on the two of them, and she is floating on air.

Sybille Malinowski does not want to wake up, not for anything in the world. Like an old horse reluctant to leave its stall, she is balking.

"Sybille, we've got money, we're independent. We can fulfill all our dreams!" A dream. Ha! This is supposed to be a dream? Swaying through the knight's hall in the arms of a young nobleman, that is a dream! Even if the aristocrat has lost everything he ever possessed in the East and the knight's hall is only a public boarding school dining hall with its furniture removed. Sybille knew this, even at the age of sixteen. The reality did not matter, since she was living her dream.

Everything here is a pale imitation, mass merchandise, clearance goods. In the past, cruises had style. This here is... the words fail her... absurd. Absurd and depressing. She tugs the back of her lounge chair upright, a movement that costs her an eternity.

What is going on? Why are they making such a racket? She is alone in the roped-off area reserved for the suite guests, with its good view of the pool and the area in front of it. The musicians have stopped playing, and that horrible competition in which the half-naked proletarians make fools of themselves is also over, thankfully. She had closed her eyes and been forced to use earplugs. Otherwise, she probably would have started screaming, not that she can even do that anymore.

Imagine you are helplessly exposed to such a situation. You cannot get away or call for help. In your mind, you stand up; perhaps you are already over there, on the way down to your cabin. But your foot is stuck here and refuses to turn. Won't turn just ninety degrees, to let me stand up. I scream, but only incoherent babbling emerges from my mouth, which remains pointed at the floor anyway because I can no longer lift my neck. *Babbling.*

People think that I'm crazy, a prattling creature in a wheelchair. However, my mind is crystal clear. I see, hear, understand everything, perhaps more sharply and acutely than I ever have in my entire life, because all that remains are my thoughts.

Humility, Sybille. Be humble and grateful for the Mediterranean sun that warms you, for the places you can still visit, for the people who are around you.

Grateful? You talking to me, Parkinson's? You talking to me? Frau Malinowski, if you please. That is what you should call me. I never was one for familiarities.

So what is this racket? And why are they all standing over there at the railing?

Sybille—no, Frau Malinowski—cannot see well because of all the people.

Dolphins again? Something else must have happened. The ship is not moving, and the music has stopped. They are always playing music here, day and night, either live or over the speakers. Unbearably loud, horrible music. What is going on? Hello?

The girl from the security team does not hear me, nobody does. Where is she going in such a hurry? She has beautiful hair, like silk. Her face looks Indian, or is it Mongolian? I think she is pretty. I was pretty once, too.

That is quite a crowd at the railing. I do not want to get stuck in it with my wheelchair. Where is my water bottle? I am supposed to drink a lot. Oh yes, that's better. Something must be going on! The man with the red hair and the crew cut has been filming the whole time. Now he is looking over at me. If only I—if only he could show me what he is recording.

Ulrich also liked to film things. Narrow film, I think they called it Super 8. We traveled to so many conferences, always meeting the same people in similar hotels, whether in Japan or Mexico. Striking off on your own was not all that easy, especially for women.

On the Baltic in the summer, skiing in the winter, the same thing year in, year out. It was nice for the children, no doubt, and my husband could relax. But my heart was often heavy.

Wiltrud was right about that: I would have preferred to travel to cities, and I should be grateful that I can do that now. These cruises are real godsends for those of us in wheelchairs. We start in Hamburg and ultimately land in Monaco. I have to suffer through only one flight and am spared the search for a hotel that is handicapped accessible.

But that is the beauty of it, isn't it? To stroll along the lanes of a foreign city, drifting, until you find a small inn with a garden overrun by wild ivy. To clamber up a steep staircase, to sip a cup of coffee in an enchanted little nook.

Instead... have you ever descended on a city with three thousand other people, like a swarm of locusts? The locals set everything out in their shop windows, like oblations, anything that can be sold: trinkets, folklore, kitsch. Just so we can swoop down on it and then vanish as quickly as possible back on to our ship, but only after we have plucked everything bare. We are not guests whom anyone would welcome, to whom beautiful and valuable items are offered. We are like a storm that you have to weather. Plants may need the rain, but nobody welcomes its arrival. Each time we board the *Spirit of Europe*, I feel more sordid. I do not want to be connected with this monstrosity. Not me.

Sybille won't leave the ship at Palma de Mallorca. It won't matter to Wiltrud. She grew tired of pushing the wheelchair through the heat up steep lanes a long time ago.

Sybille had been surprised to learn her sister had a gambling addiction. Over the years, you turn into strangers, growing apart.

She has to go to the bathroom, but Wiltrud is playing bingo. The smallest things have become major problems. She has to practice being patient. She has to learn to ask for help.

SPIRIT OF EUROPE | DECK 4

Nikhil Mehta

Juhu Beach, Mumbai. At sunset, the air is laden with the heavy smell of oil for frying *panipuri*. Incense sticks and jasmine, threaded into the women's braids. The air hums with all the languages of the Indian subcontinent and hundreds of dialects, sprinkled with English and other components of the diaspora. Slot machines blink and spit out the future for people who want to believe that robots divine their fates. As a security guard, you find yourself in a never-ending nightmare. Just imagine, an imminent attack, and you have to locate the assassin: young, inconspicuous, Muslim. Of course! Just say it. Every one of them is a suspect. Mother India, stand by us.

Deck 4, the lower outer deck, overflows with people, reminds him of Juhu Beach on a Friday night. Slowly but forcefully, Nike pushes himself through the mass of pink bodies. They have a strong odor, the Europeans, of sweat, suntan lotion, and alcohol, despite the fact that on this ship they use more water than a midsized town in India. Like a herd, they surge forward. Having seen enough, the first row makes its way back. Attention spans are short: on average, they stare at the rubber raft for about thirty seconds. Dolphins normally keep their interest longer, but only when they appear in large groups. "Look, someone's waving!"

Some wave back.

A fat woman looks at him, her gaze brushing over his uniform and toned body. She briefly checks her reflection in his mirrored sunglasses, as she pushes her fake blond hair out of her face. "Excuse me, officer!" Her voice is faded. Those who are not already alcoholics join the club once on board, as they are downright bombarded with drink offers. Alcohol costs extra, and every extra counts in Miami.

Smile. "Yes, ma'am?"

"Officer"—fluttering her eyelids—"are we taking these... these Africans on board?"

"No, ma'am. We're waiting for the coast guard to arrive."

She nods, relieved. "You know, officer, they might be armed. Imagine if they were carrying swords..." She opens her eyes wide.

"Don't worry, ma'am." Nike momentarily rests his hand on her arm and feels her shiver. "Nothing will happen to you."

Another scrutinizing look, but she seems to have calmed down. Anything but panic right now—that security scenario is far worse than a few rusty swords. Those are way down on the list. At the top: A deadly virus. An actual terrorist attack. Fire.

Move on.

Nike walks on, radioing his team that all is well on the upper decks, people are already starting to lose interest. He calls the bridge. The old man is finally there. With all due respect, the passengers want to hear the voice of their captain right now, not one of the young guns.

"Get him to make an announcement," Nike barks at the duty officer. "Anything."

Move on.

The loudspeakers crackle. The captain has an idiotic German accent that he has been cultivating for decades, although everyone knows he has a house in Miami, but the guests love it. It makes them feel safe, just like the constant repetition.

"Ladies and gentlemen, this is your captain, Björn-Helmut Krüger, speaking from the bridge. Today, on this day at sea, we have a special highlight for you." Bingo! He announces the final round of bingo. Nice move. That will get people away from the railing. Greed trumps curiosity.

Move on.

Nike casts a parting glance over the emptying deck and disappears through a door labeled FOR CREW ONLY, taking the stairs down to the sick bay. The guests are given the impression that there is something like a hospital here, but in reality, the section consists of two quarantine units and the profitable onboard pharmacy. Whenever an operation or intensive care is absolutely necessary, they quietly remove the patient at the next port, ideally along with the relatives. Nobody wants to experience human tragedy up close, not on their vacation.

He walks straight to the cabin designated for patients with contagious diseases. The young female doctor, from somewhere in the Baltic countries, is wearing a protective mask. Panic flickers in the eyes above it. "He was lashing out. I had to tie him down."

The frail Arab is lying on the white sheets and mumbling incoherently. He is emaciated, although they have been feeding him up in the crew canteen.

Nike gently slaps him on the cheek. What was this Syrian's name again? "Marwan! Wake up!"

Shakily, the doctor's hand takes the pulse. This is something different from some old codger who's suffered a heart attack or a broken arm. "I'm afraid he has a brain hemorrhage."

Again, with the beseeching look. Nike does not have to ask, since he already knows what this means. After all, as head of security, you do more than just take a first aid course. The emergency plan reels off in his mind: the closest port is Palma de Mallorca, not reachable before tomorrow morning.

Too late.

First, call a helicopter and have him flown out to Alicante or Almería. That will cost a fortune, not to mention the operation.

Miami will hold him responsible.

The end of his career. Urmila and the children need him. The flat in Andheri West is not paid off yet. And Mumbai's property taxes are rising. School fees. The two nannies and the cook. The car. The chauffeur. His fitness studio.

Wait a moment.

Still no email from India.

Today. Surely it will come today.

He can feel it.

His karma.

"I'll take care of this." Nike has to think, but not with this woman here, who looks like she is going to pass out any minute. "No worries, Doctor."

How often does he say that? No worries. Ma'am, don't you worry, the weather will surely get better. Sir, no worries, the cargo ship over there isn't too close to us. No worries, we won't run aground. We won't sink. We won't be attacked by pirates. They are calling the bridge. They are tugging at the sleeves of his uniform. They are disrupting his work. They are writing to Miami. They are exchanging comments on their forums. They know everything better. Better than Nikhil Mehta, a.k.a. Mr. Fix-It.

His father had started out with a small cricket supplies shop, and that is where his nickname came from. Who in India had real Nikes before the economic liberalization? It was a large monotonous country without choices, without ambitions.

Now his family owns a sporting goods store in Ahmedabad's largest shopping mall. His older brother manages the company. He knows how to leverage his contacts to make a profit, and soon he will open a second store.

Nike slips out of the room. He needs space to think, to run through scenarios. The best place is the casino, since it is still empty this time of day. He sprints up the stairs. No problem, you have to work on keeping fit whenever you can. Nike spends every spare minute doing this. The fitness room for the crew is on the shoddy side, given that every last dishwasher works out there. But as a senior officer, Nike has access to the Emerald Spa: weight room, top-quality machines, treadmill with a view of the endless horizon. The whirlpool is only for passengers, but Nike does not waste time on that sort of junk anyway. Action is his credo. Keep moving. He was the one who started pickup basketball games for the crew, a chance to let off some steam after-hours, and it feels great to get slapped on the back, just one of the gang. Head of security is a lonely job; you can use all the allies you can get.

There is no comparison, however, with the regimen he follows at the club when he's back home, focusing on a different muscle group each day. In depth, A to Z. Trains his reflexes at the sandbag. Stocks up on protein snacks—you need those if you are a strict vegetarian. Urmila is happy when he ducks out of the house for a couple of hours. That is her sphere: the kitchen, the staff, the children. Nike is almost always glad when the ten weeks of vacation are over. A man like him needs challenges.

This situation is one. First rule: Never let them see you sweat. The head of security stays calm in any situation. He is a role model. The multihued LED lights draw Nike into the semidarkness as he strolls into the casino. On sea days, it is open all day long, but now it is virtually empty. The gambling addicts have been lured to the final round of bingo; the jackpot beckons. A very young pair is seated at the blackjack table, Russian oligarch kids from the Royal Suite. She is wearing a very short black skirt above thin white legs and extremely high heels. Above, a girlish face with hamster cheeks that makeup cannot quite conceal. He appears bloated beneath his designer shirt—not enough exercise. Either it is still puppy fat or the coke is already at work. Still, they giggle like teenagers, while the dealer pulls in their chips. Guests to Nike's liking. They don't cause trouble and have limitless cash at their disposal.

Nike takes off his sunglasses and looks around. He can't help it; he has to check. Always. Everywhere. The corners. The mirrors on the wall. Nothing unusual. Good.

Move on.

He patrols the deserted rows of slot machines. Their noises compete for his attention, whistle at him like men catcalling a pretty lady. His thoughts keep churning. Problem: Illegal person on board, brain injury, emergency. Security level: Red. Imminent threat to Nikhil Mehta's future. He runs through the possible consequences of this predicament. His thoughts whizz back and forth. Almería. Palma. Miami.

Sheila McGuire, corporate head of security, has been watching him since May. Professional, but markedly less friendly than before. "Solve the problem, Nikhil. I do my job, you do yours." In the beginning, she had answered his emails: *I'll take care of it.* With a period. Then an exclamation mark. Then nothing. For a few weeks now, there has been radio silence between Sheila and Nikhil. *Solve the problem. You're the head of security. That's what we pay you for.* Miami won't get involved. There were two, maybe three attempts to get the higher-ups involved, if any.

The problem is getting the illegals off the boat once you have transported them from one country to another. In this case, Spain. The Syrian had wanted to leave the ship in Barcelona anyway; the Nigerian had not cared. So send both off with the Guardia Civil. But the Spaniards had said: "Nada. Take them to Malta where you picked them up." The Maltese had more than enough on their hands and had not wanted them either. Neither had the Brits at the turnover in Southampton. And Miami is out of the question. To the Americans, it was better to keep these guys on board than to let them set foot on sacred US soil. *Solve it, Mehta. Find a solution!* A nice, shitty mess.

Nikhil reins in his thoughts. Slow down, go through your options. The Arab must leave the ship. Immediately.

The casino has large portholes with heavy velvet curtains pulled back at the middle. They keep it nicely dim here. Nike steps toward the round window that just barely clears the water line.

At eye level, very far away, the raft is dancing on the waves.

Disappears.

Reappears.

Disappears.

Move on.

AIRWAVES

Salvamento Marítimo:	Sir?
Spirit of Europe:	Yes, sir, go ahead for *Spirit of Europe*. This is the captain speaking.
Salvamento Marítimo:	Are these people requesting any help from your side?
Spirit of Europe:	Yes, sir. We are wondering: Will you be able to send a boat out and pick up the refugees at this current position or would you like us to pick them up?
Salvamento Marítimo:	There is an alternative, sir, that you wait in this area until we're able to send a search-and-rescue unit to the area.
Spirit of Europe:	How long will that take, sir? How long will it take for the rescue unit to get to this area?

Salvamento Marítimo: At this moment, we don't have a clear picture of the situation, but it should be approximately one hour. We'll send a high-speed boat.

Spirit of Europe: Repeat please: When will you be able to deploy the fast boat?

Salvamento Marítimo: We estimate about an hour or an hour and a half.

Spirit of Europe: Is that one and a half hours to get to this position or to deploy from the land station?

Salvamento Marítimo: No, to reach your current location.

Spirit of Europe: Okay, sir, we will stay in this area and wait for the rescue team.

Salvamento Marítimo: Okay, please keep visual contact with the small boat. We'll keep you informed about the developments of the—of the ETA of the rescue unit to the area.

Spirit of Europe: Okay, thank you very much. Standing by 27. We will keep visual contact with the refugees in the boat.

SIOBHAN OF IRELAND | ENGINE DECK

Oleksij Lewtschenko

Olek presses the green button. With a belch, the *Siobhan* wakes up from her nap.

"Come on, old girl."

Another routine glance over the instruments.

He trusts his ears more than the devices. The control room is air-conditioned; however, the door to the engine room cracks just barely before the heat and noise assault him. No one, except Olek, lingers there longer than necessary. He loves the smell of diesel oil. His father had serviced the ship engines for the Black Sea Fleet.

The Black Sea Fleet: historically part of the Russian navy. Since the eighteenth century, the fleet's center for operations in the Black Sea and the Mediterranean has been Sevastopol, Crimea.

In 1990, Olek joined the fleet as a sailor. His father, the old mechanical engineer, could not have been prouder. With the collapse of the Soviet Union in '91, the Soviet fleet suddenly found itself floating in Ukrainian waters. Initially the two countries said fifty-fifty, but Yeltsin was too greedy to make do with that. The Russians wanted the whole fleet. So he threatened to cut off our gas supply, and voilà, it turned into eighty-twenty. Does this ring a bell? Don't say it out loud, just think it. You are still allowed to do that.

Normally he enjoys the brutal heat down here, but today he is not feeling well. His head buzzes.

The stairs, shortness of breath.

Deck B: crew's mess, officers' mess.

Not hungry.

Deck C: crew quarters.

Deck D: master deck.

Out into the fresh air where Olek's spot is located, way back here. It is his own tiny piece of the ship, perhaps two meters square, sheltered from the wind. White railing, green planks, and a bench painted blue. Blue was all that was left.

He sits down on the bench, pulls out his tobacco, and rolls a cigarette. He listens to the pistons chug evenly in strict time. It has a strong heart, the *Siobhan*.

Finally allowing his eyes to focus, he stands back up and looks down over the railing. Someone is hanging there on a rope, painting. They nod at each other. Olek lifts his gaze to the horizon. They are almost out of the bay, and in the distance hovers the panorama of the city between the hills.

Cartagena: the Spanish military harbor is known by a variation of its Phoenician name, Carthage. Hannibal. Later the Romans came, and soon followed their amphitheater. You really should take a look at it, instead of blowing half the morning once again on the computer...

Oh, shit. Olek has to go back in.

Rushes down the stairs. His quarters are on Deck A. In emergencies, he has to be able to reach his engine quickly. Dim twilight. Containers right in front of his window. Where is his phone?

Up the stairs. How many times has he run into something? He stopped counting at some point. His second engineer approaches—a talented boy, has a way with engines—and smiles. "Chief. How's it going?" The Filipinos are always friendly.

Back outside now. Short of breath. What's wrong today? Has to be the weather. Something's coming.

He pulls out the prepaid card and punches the code into his phone. Dmitri brought him the card from the city earlier on. Spanish radio network. The sea network is too slow to upload his pictures, which are all high-res, only best quality.

His passions: Wikipedia. Facebook. VesselFinder Pro. ShipSpotting.com. Of course, most of the spotters are unemployed landlubbers with nothing better to do. They stand around the harbor with their telephoto lenses, pointing their cameras as you put to sea. The poor sods have to take whatever comes their way. Olek is an Elite Spotter. Username: Cosmochief. Two hundred forty-three ships, from supertankers to sailing yachts. Excellent ratings. He clicks through his photo library.

There is his last picture: the Libyan freighter in Algiers Harbor, where it has been docked for months, good only for scrapping at this point. He caught it in full profile, the rust glowing nicely in the evening light. The crew has to be on the verge of starvation, waiting like Easter lambs for someone to come and release them. They simply don't get it that their country is sinking, as they slaughter one another on both sides.

That is where we will all end up if things keep going this way.

Don't think about it.

But still, images flash in his mind.

The steps of Odessa. *Battleship Potemkin* (Russian title: Броненосец Потёмкин). The world-famous silent film from Sergei Eisenstein premiered on December 21, 1925, at the Moscow Bolshoi Theatre as the official anniversary film for the celebration of the 1905 Russian Revolution. The plot was loosely based on actual events that took place the year of the revolution: the mutiny of the crew against the czarist officers on the Russian battleship *Knjas Potjomkin Tawritsch-eski.*

The mosaic at Katerynyns'ka Square, high up under crumbling stucco. Catherine II, known as Catherine the Great (Russian: Екатерина Алексеевна), became empress of Russia in 1762—the only female monarch to be awarded the epithet "the Great" by the history books. Representative of enlightened absolutism, she founded Odessa in 1794 as a military outpost on the Black Sea.

Olek the boy often plays in front of that house; they live right around the corner. A sailor shuffles by, looks up at the mosaic, and crosses himself quickly. Once the old man rounds the corner, the boy makes the same gesture. She sends a tingle down his spine, this woman in the mosaic. Blessed Virgin Mary, protect our homeland and loved ones. Looking exhausted but determined, sitting in the midst of rubble and tank chains, she holds the trumpet in her left hand and the royal scepter in her right. She is like Odessa, which embodies the spirit of Catherine the Great: powerful, destructive, provocative. A city like a high. Back in the day, it was the soft, beguiling high of opium; today, it is *shirka*, the heroin knockoff cooked up from poppy straw, extremely addictive. Quick high with a hard crash, its popularity soared in Ukraine after the collapse of the Soviet Union. Brutal stuff. Odessa, Saint Catherine, you have broken me, all this back and forth with the fleet. Which fatherland am I actually serving?

Once again, he is standing in front of the house on Katerynyns'ka Square; now he is twenty-one. Irina is forcing him to choose between her and the *shirka*. He is standing under the chestnut tree, freezing. There is now a Mexican food place where there used to be a bakery. Behind him, a souped-up BMW thunders past. Odessa's wealthy are living high in this new age, while the unemployed and the drug-addicted are crashing and burning. Olek prays to the woman in the mosaic; nothing else comes to him.

She is the protectress of sailors. Olek signs up, seeking refuge in the warm cave of an engine room. He trains to be a mechanic and enrolls in the academy three years later.

He catalogs every ship with its name and IMO code, now uploading the picture of the *Spirit of Europe* from last night, emerging from the fog like the *Titanic* in front of the iceberg. It was downright eerie, but the photo will get him five stars, guaranteed. Damn it! The internet has crashed again. Where is the coast? They are now out on open ocean, the Escombreras Refinery to portside. He had recently read about it on Wikipedia. It is huge.

He holds his phone over the railing. Just don't let it fall. All right, upload complete. The painter down below waves again.

Olek pockets his phone, tosses a final glance over the railing. Out of the corner of his eye: something was just there. Plastic? The entire sea is going under in that stuff. He read in *Science* that eight million tons of it land in the oceans each year, microplastic and other degraded material collecting into ocean gyres. In mid-2014, off the coast of Hawaii's Big Island, geologists discovered formations comprising melted synthetic material, volcanic stone, coral fragments, and grains of sand. Because of its solidity, they described it as a form of rock, calling it a plastiglomerate. The world is drowning in plastic. Anyone traveling over open ocean can see that we're all heading down the drain, one way or the other.

Olek moves toward the stern. Is that a piece from a boat? Keeps walking. No, not a boat. Hair. Black hair in dreadlocks

He throws his arms up.

"Dmitri, stop! Stop!"

Dashing back, he takes the exterior stairs up to Deck E, heaving open the heavy iron door to the bridge. "A person!" Wheezing. "Dmitri, stop!" A corpse, a man or woman. Olek crosses himself. Another one already.

The first mate is playing container dominoes on the computer. Jumping up, he glances at the captain, grabs the binoculars, and rushes out. A good lad, Sergei. Meanwhile Olek and Dmitri stand, frozen in place. Neither moves. Neither says a word.

Sergei comes back in. "Couldn't see anything, Captain. Stop the engines?"

Dmitri ignores him, steps closer and grasps Olek by the shoulders. "Chief!"

Olek inhales. "Dmitri, we have to stop!"

"Calm down, Olek." Dmitri does not drop his arms as he studies him. "Are you sure he is still alive? Olek? Are you sure?"

Still alive? How should he know? It was so fast, a moment, then over. Olek shakes his head. No, he is not sure.

"Do you know what it costs to stop the engines? To go back? Do you know what that costs?" Dmitri shakes him, just slightly. Olek exhales, and Dmitri lets him go but keeps his hands raised just in case. "Was anyone else on deck?"

Olek shakes his head. The Filipino painter had been looking in the other direction.

"Maybe you just saw a piece of plastic tarp. Olek?"

Dmitri looks at him. Sergei looks at him.

Olek nods.

Crosses himself again.

First, the corpse in Oran, and now a drowning victim.

A second omen.

Olek has goose bumps.

And Dmitri? Dmitri takes the binoculars from the first officer and looks out ahead, the containers forming a pattern of rectangles against the sea.

Sergei sits back down at the computer.

"A storm's coming," Dmitri says, carefully placing the binoculars on the ledge next to the coffee canister, before going to the table in the back that holds the sea maps.

Olek does not move. Dmitri walks back over. "Everything all right, chief engineer?" He hands him an envelope. "This should take your mind off things. There was mail from home waiting for you in Cartagena."

The radio crackles. "Sea Rescue Cartagena. Sea Rescue Cartagena to *Spirit of Europe*. Can you hear me? Copy."

SANTA FLORENTINA

Diego Martínez

The purse seine forms an almost perfect circle in the water. The round area contrasts strongly with the surrounding water, its blue duller and more sluggish than the powerful azure of the rest of the sea. It can't be real, though, since a fishing net is actually porous, with the same water in as well as out. And yet... It must have something to do with the refraction of the light.

Diego chokes the motor at the very moment the circle fills out. In that same instant, his father flips the switch and begins to haul in the net. They wait as the noonday heat burns down on them. Diego's gaze sweeps across the coast: Cabo de Agua and, beyond it, the Bay of El Gorguel. He spent endless summer afternoons clambering around up there. With the rest of his family down on the beach, grilling, Diego would find a sunny spot among the rocks, book in hand.

He would have hardly opened the pages when he saw them: the British frigates *Minerve* and *Blanche*, under the command of the later Lord Nelson, engaged in a bitter sea battle against the Spanish frigates *San Sabina*, *Ceres*, *Perla*, and *Matilda*. The *San Sabina* would have already fallen into English hands. The cannon thunder and smoke hung over the Bay of Cartagena. Then out of the haze, a frigate materialized. At the last second, General Juan Contreras with the *Nu-*

mancia came to the rescue. The artillery from the batteries at Cabo Tiñoso roared from the coastline. And the tide turned...

In his cozy spot between the boulders, little Diego could not have cared less about the fact that Contreras wasn't even alive in 1799, the year Nelson was floating off the coast of Cartagena, and that the powerful cannons on the hill were first placed there over a century later. "Kaboom!" he bellows as he hurls a stone toward the sea. *"Hasta luego, Señor Nelson!"*

The reel hauling in the net locks in place with a snap. Still smiling at the thought of the numerous battles he fought as boy, Diego turns toward his father. Together they wrest their catch on board. Shimmering mackerel flop around on the floor of the *Santa Florentina*. It is not all that many. His father works quickly and focused, while Diego grabs for a fish, but it slithers between his fingers. He curses under his breath. The hand movements he learned as a boy, before he could even write, seem to be gradually fading from his memory. He is suddenly overwhelmed by a sense of irretrievability.

His father had stubbornly insisted that there were schools of mackerel at Cabo de Agua. Perhaps they had been there a day or two ago. An old fisherman can sense such things. But the large fishing fleets use helicopters to locate the schools, and by the time the inshore fishermen arrive, everything's gone.

"Can you take the wheel?" The old man heaves the box of fish into the cabin. He flees from the view of what lies beyond Isla de Escombreras, even after all the many years. Diego stands at the doorway and adjusts the tiller with his foot. That is how the fishermen in the Martínez family do it. They couldn't care less about the safety uproar. The Virgen de la Caridad of Escombreras is the only one watching out for them.

Diego likes to cook. In a seafood cookbook, he'd once read that the ancient Romans had a sauce that was their version of ketchup. It was made from fermented mackerel and was called *garum*. The best garum sociorum was made far from Rome, on the outer edges of the empire, in a small village near the harbor city of Cartagena. In Latin, mackerel were called *scomber*, and that's why the Romans named the place Escombreras. This is Diego's favorite version of the story, lost over the course of the centuries and reappearing in a cookbook.

In Spanish, though, *escombreras* only means "dump site." Diego involuntarily glances to his right. On this side, the island is no longer an island; it is a connector to the new harbor basin. As if drawn with a ruler, the concrete quay stretches out toward the sea. Day and night, tankers load and unload here, while freighters are filled with black slag that they transport God knows where. The old village is gone except for the ruins of the church, which stubbornly rear up between the spherical tanks. Four saints, along with the Virgen de la Caridad, used to ornament the church. One of them had been Santa Florentina, for whom his grandfather had named this boat. Instead of the plateau on which the cross had once stood, a bizarre terraced landscape now exists, as if a monster had bitten a giant block of stone out of the mountain.

"Farther that way," his father hollers from within.

Diego adjusts his course. It's chilly. Repsol, the Spanish oil multinational, is an empire of darkness. A hazy veil permanently hangs over the valley. The gas flares with their nervous flickering, the bloated tanks, the toxic waste dumps. They are like an ulcer that has spread across his family's homeland and devoured it. Like the ulcer that is causing his father to waste away, eating him from the inside out. On his days off, Diego goes out with him. No one knows how much longer this will go on.

During that summer of 1969, the tanks burned for eight days and nights, as the wind drove the flames closer and closer to the village. On the ninth night, the residents gave up. After two thousand years of fishing, the fishermen became company employees who transported slag and building materials in their boats. The company paid good money and built them their own neighborhood in Cartagena, apartments with water and power. Repsol is the future. Several from the second generation, including Diego's father, tried to pick fishing back up again, but it was too late. If there had ever been another future, it died with the village. Dead and buried.

Their last fish trap is far out by the Cala Cortina. Since Diego is always on call, they set out their permanently anchored nets within a thirty-minute radius from Cartagena, a condition the Martínezes are willing to accept in order to no longer be reliant on the cannery's price pressure. Diego heads toward the black flag that marks the trap. Perhaps they have caught at least a couple of rock lobsters. Diego's younger brother waits tables at Club Nautico, and they always need extra lobsters there. His father comes out of the cabin, refusing to look toward Escombreras. He steps nimbly across the narrow boards up to the bow. He will not be needing a walker any time soon.

"Ho!"

Diego reacts instantly to the quiet call. The sound of the motor dies away, as the *Florentina* glides soundlessly toward the trap. Something has been caught in it. His father saw it right away. No word passes between them; no need for it.

Silence.

Wind.

Together they pull him on board. It takes only one look for Diego to know that the boy is beyond all help. This is his fifth year working for the sea rescue service in Cartagena. How many bodies has he already drawn out of the water? No idea. He is not one who holds on to misfortune by keeping count. The first body is always the worst. For him, it was two: a French couple on their honeymoon with a kayak. You eventually get used to it, are happy for every living one you fish out of the water. The world is the way it is. We are all caught in the crisis, and his job is secure. The more people who need his help, the more secure it is.

That's just the way it is.

The boy here probably came from one of the *pateras*, the rafts. Over the past year, they have been crossing up here, because Frontex's drones and radar have been covering more and more of the area from Gibraltar to the north. And they are getting younger and younger. Diego watches his father's back as he bends over the dead body.

Without warning, the lump in his throat swells, then something bursts.

In astonishment, he hears his own sobs as they burst out, loud and strong, against the jagged rocks of Costa Blanca.

COASTAL ROAD NEAR ESCOMBRERAS | SPAIN

Zohra Hamadi

Zohra's in high spirits. She's actually done it. She took her brother's car and drove it to Spain. It is fifteen hours to Almería if you avoid the toll roads, according to the route planner on her phone. It hasn't worked out quite like that: she has been traveling for almost twenty-four hours, snatching a few hours' sleep here and there. Zohra had figured the trip would take longer. Before today, she's never driven farther than the supermarket with the kids, and once a couple of kilometers on the road between the ferry in Oran and Sidi Bel Abbès. She also wondered if her back would hold up for the journey, since it was so soon after the last round of rehab. But it has. Maybe her body has finally grown used to the pain.

Would you believe it? The courts have just decided that she is healthy enough to live in Algeria, and now she does actually feel better. "Are you serious?" Zohra asked the female judge. "I should continue my treatment in Algeria? Not even the president lets himself be treated in Algeria." They'd all laughed, everyone in courtroom 305 of the district court in Marseille North, Department for Residency Permits for Foreigners, the judge most of all. Then she had announced that Zohra would be deported if she could not prove that she had a permanent job within one month. That had been six weeks ago, and obviously she hadn't been able to find a job that quickly.

She drives through the brown mountains, the sudden bleakness of her surroundings dampening her spirits. It is scary here, an abandoned lunar landscape. No oncoming traffic. The jolly vacation chaos of La Mancha, just a couple of kilometers behind her, is nowhere to be seen. Ancient walled chimneys protrude from the brown earth.

The voice of her satnav is too loud. "Take the second exit at the traffic circle toward Cartagena."

Around the next bend appears a futuristic jumble of shiny steel pipes. The plant is dazzling in its shades of green, yellow, and red, and in between, spiked pyramids of black dust trickle down from conveyor belts. Trucks with tarps hiding their cargoes drive in and out. One of them cuts her off, wedging itself directly in front of her. Zohra hits the brakes hard.

Where am I?

Gas. Round tanks. Pipes, now running along both sides of the road. A refinery. Memories of Algeria pop up. Arzew. Oran. Along the coast. Where is the ocean?

Another traffic circle.

More pipes.

Without using its blinker, the truck in front of her takes a sharp right and frees up the view. The entire valley is a single refinery, whose bundles of pipes run right down to the harbor, almost man-high in diameter. Next to the road, workers in overalls and helmets are sitting on the pipes, taking a cigarette break. This is almost the exact moment she catches the biting smell of gas.

Her hands clutch the steering wheel; her entire body tightens. Just get away from the gas. Her mother had been scared even before the man came to change the cartridge in the kitchen. Zohra, a young girl back then, had hidden herself back in the far corner of the overgrown garden, near the olive trees.

Another traffic circle. The Renault Espace skids around the bend. She must drive more slowly. Beneath her to the left, a massive flame flickers out of a high chimney, swathing everything in a cloud of smoke and haze. Behind it, tankers are docked in the inner harbor against blocks of concrete.

Which side of the ocean am I on? This could well be Algeria.

A tunnel.

Zohra drives in. The tunnel is too dark for sunglasses, but it's just for a short moment. It's already getting light again up ahead. She slows down, and a truck honks behind her. The lights in the rear mirror blind her, and it will only take a moment before it will be riding her bumper. And then? Without papers? The owner of the car unreachable?

She emerges from the tunnel, sees a parking area out of the corner of her eye, and pulls over. The trunk lays on its horn and thunders past. She turns off the car, hands shaking.

Pull yourself together, Zohra, it's not far now.

Only now does she see that, below her, the sea runs into a small bay. Parasols are packed in close. Families are picnicking, and people are standing in the water, chatting. It is as if the gas refinery on the other side of the tunnel was just a bad dream, an illusion. She allows her gaze to wander languidly out to the sea. An old fishing boat is bobbing between two poles over there, as two men pull in their nets. *Tranquillo*, the Spanish say, whenever she tries to order a coffee. Everything is *tranquillo* here.

Two days ago, Zohra was also *tranquillo*. Lonely, yes, but you can dream. Then the call from Karim's mother, who can't understand why her son's fiancée insists on living in France, instead of with her future husband in Algeria. The constant reproach in her voice, usually concealed, was out in the open this time. "He is on his way again." *To be with you.* She didn't say it, but Zohra knew she was thinking it.

Even though he promised Zohra he would wait until she has a job and a resident's permit, until she can finally get him to join her. "Then we'll get married, my darling, *inshallah*." Only Karim is not the sort of man who waits. He doesn't let other people tell him what to do. He needs to be with his fiancée as she waits around, on her own in France. To protect her. To get a job. To finally have a normal life: apartment, car, work, kids. These dreams are the ones shared by everyone in the neighborhood La Solidarité, Marseille, Fifteenth Arrondissement. On the weekends, they head to the beach at La Redonne. The children build castles in the sand, as the men show off their muscles and the women their beauty.

People from Algeria, like Zohra, like her brother, like her cousins. They have all gone home for the summer vacation; only Zohra had to stay behind. If she goes now, she can't come back.

"Stay there," her parents said. "We sacrificed everything so that you could get to France for your back treatment."

"Stay there," Karim said. "I will come to you. Algeria has no future."

She is alone in Marseille. The high-rises are deserted. Makes coffee. Gets all the keys together. Day after day, the same tour through the empty apartments, one after the other. Get the mail, water the flowers, air the place. Outdoors, the heat kills her whenever she walks around between the empty houses. She misses the children: two nephews, one niece. She normally spends her time with them while her brother and his wife are at work. Now the days are endless.

"Almería," Karim's mother said. "That is where he will go ashore at night. He will call you as soon as he is there."

Zohra wants to surprise Karim. That is why she took the car keys and set off, toward Karim. He will not arrive before dark. The drive ahead of her should take less than two hours.

Almost there. No rush now.

She suddenly feels an irresistible urge to go and sit with the people on the beach, to pretend that she is part of them. To pretend that this is La Redonne. She needs only to go down there, and her family would be already waiting.

Zohra opens the door, gets out carefully. First one foot, then the other. She stands up. The pain hits her immediately, like a knife in the back. She tries to remember the breathing exercises the doctor taught her.

Panic, all alone in this foreign country.

Breathe in. Breathe out.

Merde, damn. Tears shoot to her eyes.

She cannot drive on.

Breathe.

She is drawn to the people, almost instinctively. The scoliosis forces her to hunch her back over like an old woman. She slowly limps down the path that leads to the bay. Breathe in. Breathe out. Breathe in. Step by step. An eternity. Finally there.

The sea laps lazily on the beach. Two blond children, identical, crouch in the waves. One gets up and comes toward her, holding out a spade to her. Zohra's cell phone rings.

RAFT (NO NAME)

Karim Yacine

Allah, why are you doing this to me?

Why? Until now, he has never wrangled with fate, has simply trusted God. And now, on this crossing, this trust is shattering, piece by piece, like a glass dome under which he has spent his entire life up to now. The glass is no longer holding together, as it rains thousands of tiny splinters into the sea, revealing the merciless sun.

He feels finished.

Karim wipes his forehead.

Am I going crazy?

The night was reluctant to end, out there in the fog. It was hours till Karim actually knew where he was heading, so he just kept going, until dawn broke, somewhere off to his right. He'd corrected his course, saying nothing to the others. They had always had enough gas before, when he followed a direct course. Eventually it was light, and Abdelmjid divided the dates for breakfast. Slowly the men's trepidation evaporated, only the cousin remained quiet, eating nothing. Who could blame him? His brother is either dead or in prison. What is worse, nobody knows.

Karim has done this five times, and he has never lost a man. Never! He made it twice without a glitch, was driven back to land by the coast guard two other times, and once, because of engine problems, was fished out by the Spanish sea rescue service. That time they had cheered, as they sat in the rescue boat. He had filmed it all with his phone and later uploaded the recording to the internet. The videos of the Harragas are cult material in Algeria. It's like an addiction, man—they get so many clicks and likes.

And yet, all the laughter from that video clip dried up the moment they reached Murcia.

And that's exactly where they will land again. If...

Karim looks over at the cruise ship. If they don't give a few liters of gas, take them on board, do something.

Abdelmjid keeps waving, like he has been doing for at least the past ten minutes. He has taken off his red scarf and is waving it back and forth like a lunatic. The others' voices drone on in his ears. One of the two boys from the neighborhood is filming everything with his phone. Yet another YouTube clip.

"Their gonna get us outta here!"

"We'll be cruising, man, too cool!"

"Huhuhu, cruiser, we're coming!"

"Shut up, all of you! Damn it, Abdelmjid, sit down! Or do you want to kill us?" He must have said it aloud because suddenly everything is quiet. Abdelmjid sits down but continues waving stubbornly.

Karim needs to think. The cruise liner has stopped. Nice. And now? What are they planning to do with us? They show no signs of giving us any gas or taking us on board.

They're waiting.

We're waiting.

Murcia, deportation prison. Three years ago, the Spanish policeman had dragged him out of the cell after a few weeks and pushed him out the door. Just like that, with nothing in his pockets, no money, no phone. "You want to get to Europe? You've got it. Go! Get out of here!" The cop had spat in the dust at Karim's feet and then whispered: "If you show up again, you'll sit here until you rot. We'll nail you for human trafficking."

Now what's going on?

Nothing's going on! They keep us here until the Guardia Civil shows up, to entertain the gawkers up there.

"Stop waving this second, Abdelmjid, or I'll throw you overboard!"

Abdelmjid stops, finally.

Kiss your future good-bye, Karim Yacine! *Salaam alaikum,* Zohra. *Salaam alaikum* to our unborn children. *Salaam alaikum,* Europe.

How late is it? How long will it take?

Karim looks at his phone and is surprised to see that it has connected to the cruise ship's mobile network. He activates the GPS.

Not far to the coast anymore, to Cartagena. It is only a few kilometers from there to Murcia. The despair drives tears to his eyes. His fingers automatically find their way over the keypad, to hear her voice one last time.

"Hello?"

She sounds so close.

"Forget about me, darling. I'm as good as dead."

SPIRIT OF EUROPE | BRIDGE

Léon Moret

They call it the ejection seat, when they are in the mood for joking. Léon isn't in the mood right now. The modern ergonomic office chair is firmly bolted to the floor, directly in front of the panorama window, its fabric cover navy blue. When it is quiet out on the water, the boy with the binoculars is allowed to sit here. Now Léon is sitting on the ejection seat, 180 degrees of blue stretching out before him. Aquamarine to sky blue. Divided into squares, big ones above, smaller ones below. Windscreen wipers are attached at irregular intervals in the top squares. There is no logic to it.

Just like the raft, bobbing up and down out there.

Not again.

It can't be. Twice in three months. How many of these damned things are drifting around the Mediterranean, breaking down right in front of his nose?

Léon has an uneasy feeling, a tugging at the back of his throat, like when you get too much MSG in your chop suey at the Chinese restaurant. He should be immune by now, considering the amount of preservatives added to the food here. Rajiv from food and beverages recently shared this information with him after a few beers. If this wasn't done, everything would rot in front of them. Germs would spread. Rajiv had shivered. "And you know, Léon, my friend, what our cruise director always says." Rajiv had gotten up, looked into the imaginary camera of Cruise TV, and shouted: "There is only one remedy against sickness on board: wash your hands, wash your hands, wash your hands!" He'd flailed around like a cheerleader, as Léon wept with laughter.

But now he has this nasty feeling, because the raft is triggering a vague memory. That is the way it is with things you mess up and can't undo: first, they flow through you hot like molten metal, then the steel solidifies and you only feel only the occasional prick. Small pangs in your insides, which don't bother you much. Things that don't carry any consequences never really happened.

Ejection seat. Nobody has relieved him yet.

Behind him, the captain is radioing alternately with Miami and Salvamento Marítimo. Don't take them on board, under any circumstances. Ah. Léon can almost hear Captain Krüger's artery swelling. "No, but we have to check at least. That's maritime law." We have to assist stranded people. Someone gives him a long speech, probably on responsibilities and insurance regulations. He finally loses his temper. The damned sea rescue service won't be here for at least an hour. He is dispatching a lifeboat now. "I don't care!" he yells. "I'm still in charge here!"

Léon smiles. So old school. Won't let himself be talked out of his convictions. Maybe he should have told the captain back then—no, it turned out all right. Best not to stir things up.

It is a good thing this raft is so far away. The other one, back in June, was right in front of the prow, in the middle of the night. They had basically thrown themselves in front of the *Europe*. They wanted to come on board. Maybe they hadn't even had a leak. You can get water inside a boat in other ways. Léon had woken the captain, and they had decided to bring the people on board. There were almost forty of them, even some women.

Nike had had quite a lot to do. He had finally been able to implement his emergency plans. Normally nothing like this happens. The people on the raft had to leave everything behind except for the clothes they were wearing. No weapons. No germs. No electronic devices that could be used as bombs. They brought them into the conference center and set up a buffet. The good life until the next harbor. Doors locked from the outside.

Léon went straight from the bridge to a party that night. One of the Eastern Europeans was celebrating his birthday, and those people celebrate longer and wilder than anyone else. They had gotten hold of the raft, hosed it down, and filled it with ice cubes to cool the vodka. That is how cynical they are. The elevator did not arrive, as is often the case. They have sex in there at night. Or whatever. So down the stairs on foot, he got the floors mixed up—everything looks the same here. In any case, he suddenly found himself outside the conference center. Nike's guard was not there, maybe in the restroom. Then he heard someone hammering against the door from the inside. "Hey, let us out! We want to go to the disco!" Léon listened. Sure, obviously they could hear it, since it was right below them, the even better life. "Hey, let us out! Just one hour." Clubbing. They'd just been fished from the middle of the ocean and this was what they were worrying about? Léon laughed. Those guys were pretty chill.

Then, once more, he can't remember. His memories pick up only after the door is already open. Two guys. High fives.

"Okay, hurry up."

"Hey, cool, man."

"You have to be back before we dock."

"Sure, man!" Victory pose to those behind them.

"Just you two."

The three of them headed down to the party, and it was pretty cool. The Nigerian was really funny. The other guy was Syrian or Iraqi or something, a bit depressed by the war down there, but that is easy to forget about if you're dancing to the Balkan beat. You can have an absolute blast. Léon can't remember how he got to bed that morning. That doesn't happen to him very often.

For once, he and Mado had the day off together and went ashore. Which harbor was it again? Probably Malta. They ate seafood and rented a convertible. That counts as our vacation, when it is just the two of us. No one requesting anything. No uniforms. No responsibility. Just some bay that none of our buses goes to. That is paradise.

When they got back to Valletta just before cast-off, the border police had already picked up the refugees. Nike was hopping mad, because one of his staff messed up the head count. He was kicked off board, without notice. Lots of excitement, lots of shouting on the pier.

Léon had not even thought about whether the two runaways had gotten back on time, and nobody ever asked him about it. The only thing he can vaguely remember is the skirmish at the party. The Nigerian got in a fight with a Romanian, shouting about all the plans he had for when he finally made it to Europe. In any case, the Romanian yelled back: "You have no idea, you fucking nigger. You'll be deported, right away!" The Nigerian wanted to head-butt him, but someone intervened, and the DJ cranked up the music.

Lalita Masarangi

Judging by the noises coming out of the stall, it's likely to take a lot longer. Lalita is standing in front of the mirror in the handicapped restrooms. The old woman intercepted her; it couldn't be helped.

Jo will have to wait.

Jo.

She leans over the sink and examines her face. They say that Gurkhas' faces show no emotion. They are 100 percent fearless. Are you fearless, Lalita? Will you be able to bear what you see when you find Jo?

Something is wrong. Very wrong.

This time you will look danger in the eye, Lalita Masarangi. You won't run off again. You are fearless. You are a Gurkha.

That time it had all been too much for her! Losing both brother and boyfriend on the same day, farewell by text message: "We're sorry, Anu." That was her older brother's nickname for her, because as a child she had always talked to Annapuma. Her father, pale and choking with rage. The sadness behind her mother's unwavering smile. Fate had wanted her to find the old newspaper that same day, on the bus en route to school in Aldershot, which was just an hour from London and the two boys who had broken her heart.

Nine hours and a whole world away from Annapuma, her mountain.

She had chosen Annapuma. The mountain has always been her secret friend, a confidant and ally for the girl from Pokhara. Nothing in the world is as powerful as the Himalayas. You have to lower your eyes when Annapuma is lit up by the sun, so bright, so unbearably bright. Mighty warrior, guarding the valley.

She wrangled a flight to Nepal out of her daddy. Then she was back with her grandparents in Pokhara, after six years in Aldershot. "You have changed, girl." They did not know her brother was gay. Only good news is passed on. Their son, her father, after fifteen years of service in the British army, was now the proud owner of his own company in England: Annapuma Security Services Limited. He had made the right decision, the son, when the Maoists seized control of the capital in 2004. "Child, child, these are uncertain times. The king has abdicated; the Maoists are in parliament."

She told the grandparents about Aldershot for hours on end: About the pensioned Gurkhas who arrived daily, after finally receiving the right of residence for themselves and their families. About the famous actress who fought for the right of the elite soldiers to live in the country they served. And about people, her neighbors, who quietly, behind her back at first, and then ever more loudly, complained about the town's decline.

There are things she did not discuss: How embarrassing the old Nepalese are who wander around town. How embarrassing it is to be part of it. How embarrassing the extra mention in social studies class is, the one about how bravely the Royal Gurkha Rifles fought for Great Britain.

This was another reason she wanted to get away.

She had brought the newspaper with her. "The Girls Who Are Fighting to Become Gurkhas." Even the trainer is mentioned in it, the one who prepares the girls in Kathmandu for the entrance exam. What are you trying to prove? she'd asked herself. That you're better than your ancestors? For two months, she waited patiently in Pokhara, until her family allowed her to enroll in the college for design in Kathmandu.

Instead of learning to draw, she trained like an animal. The requirements: fourteen pull-ups and seventy-five push-ups in a minute, seventy sit-ups in two minutes, three miles uphill in the high mountains with twenty-five kilos on your back. She has perfect eyes and hearing already. Gurkha Girl.

Strong girls she met in the gym: Maoist ex-guerrillas and daughters from middle-class families like herself. They chatted for hours, discussing all the truths they had grown up with. What if the Brits had only been making the Nepalese believe, for hundreds of years, that they were a race of warriors so that they could have cheap soldiers? Was it actually okay for a government to export young people, instead of educating them properly? On the other hand, for many of them, it was the only opportunity to make good money. Maoists also have to survive.

And above all, the question: Will they accept?

Will the Gurkhas accept women in their regiments?

After a little under a year, Lalita passed the entrance exam as the first woman ever. Wow.

Nevertheless, the Gurkha Rifles still refused to accept her, arguing that women endanger the unity of the troops. Her own people.

She was more than welcome to apply as a soldier with the regular British troops, according to the nice white colonel in the British army office. But by then, she had gone off it all. Bugger them! As British cannon fodder to Afghanistan?

Not me.

Back in Aldershot, her daddy invited her to Gurkha Villa, which serves unbeatably good *momos*, Nepalese dumplings with lots of chili. He presented her with a kukri dagger and offered her a job in his company. Not too bad.

"Ma'am, are you all right?"

The old woman remains locked inside the stall. Rumbling noises come out. Lalita hopes she makes it back into her wheelchair in one piece. She shudders at the thought of having to go in. Playing nurse is not her sort of thing.

"Shall I call someone?"

"Definitely not! My sister is at bingo."

At least she is unlocking the door from the inside now. Lalita casts a last glance in the mirror. Get the woman out quickly and then keep on searching.

In the casino.

Jo, what did you want there?

"You are a beautiful young lady." Suddenly she is right beside her, rolling up on silent wheels.

In the mirror, Lalita sees the woman's face, the head fixed to her neck all crooked and twisted, but the eyes peering up at her are very sharp and young somehow. She feels herself flush.

"No need to be embarrassed." The slender hand taps her lower arm. "Could you please flex your muscles?"

What's that all about? Well, she does it. Suddenly the fingers grip her arm, and the old woman pulls herself up to her feet. "My hair is a nightmare." With her free hand, she runs her fingers through it.

Lalita watches. The linen trousers are also askew. "May I?" She carefully places the woman's hand on the edge of the sink, so that she can support herself. Then she uses both hands to grab the waistband and tugs. "That's better."

Their eyes meet in the mirror, and they both smile. "My name is Mrs. Malinowski. And you are Ms. Masarangi." That is what it says on the name badge Lalita wears, like all other crew members. The woman nods and mumbles to herself. "....he names are similar," Lalita thinks she hears.

She bends down to better understand the soft voice. Mrs. Malinowski rustles rather than speaks.

"And now tell me what is bothering you, Ms. Masarangi." Lalita is startled.

"I have been watching you for a while, since out on deck, and just now I've heard you sigh a few times."

A little later, Lalita pushes Mrs. Malinowski back outside. She does not want to go back onto the lounger in the suite area. She is sick of lying there like a sitting duck for everyone to look at pityingly.

She turns the conversation to the refugee boat. "I was also a refugee, so I know how it feels." She is disgusted at how some people hang around and stare. "It takes those people's dignity, doesn't it, Lalita? May I call you Lalita?"

Lalita nods and continues pushing the wheelchair.

"When will we take them on board? The men out there?"

She can barely understand the soft voice. "I don't know, ma'am."

On the other side, there are masses of empty loungers. In the half shade behind the fitness area, she helps Mrs. Malinowski lie down.

She squints at her from behind tired eyes. "Go find your friend, everything else can wait. And when you have found him, don't let him go."

Lalita takes the fragile hand and presses it to her heart.

Everything else can wait.

Casino.

SPIRIT OF EUROPE | ELEVATOR (OBSERVATION LIFT)

Nikhil Mehta

He'd intercepted Lalita Masarangi in the casino running after her boyfriend during office hours—the cheek of it! Nike
makes a mental note to talk to Miami about Annapuma Security Services. Agencies for former Gurkha soldiers are spring-
ing up like mushrooms. The British army is downsizing its
units, but it cannot possibly be laying off as many elite soldiers as are flooding the security market right now.

The elevator goes first down, then back up, before stop-
ping once more on the promenade deck.

Mental note: check programming.

Nike watches Second Security Officer Masarangi, who is
staring dolefully through the window toward the stage on
the promenade. It is not difficult to guess what she is thinking of right now.

A family gets in, parents and children, all overweight and
badly mannered. Judging by the time, they have squeezed in
a snack between lunch and cake in the Café Royal. Overeat-
ing is the most common cause of heart attacks and collapses
on cruises, beating out even sunstroke and alcohol poisoning.
The children shout at each other, and Nike assumes they are
either Dutch or Belgian. The father has ketchup on his shirt;
the boy has a slice of pizza in his hand. He steps forward

to the windowpane, stares out and drops it. Nike says noth-ing—that is protocol—but the mother catches his glance and bends down with a groan to pick up her offspring's scraps. They get out on Deck 8.

Masarangi is now staring vacantly at the carpet, which today reads FRIDAY. People here forget everything, even what day it is.

"Officer!" Nike bellows. Her gaze shoots up. Good reflexes. "Prove to me that you are worth your pay. I need your full concentration now. I want you to accompany me outside." He sees protest flare up in her expression.

He needs one or two women on his team. Controls are carried out at every harbor, in and out. The Sea Pass, which replaces credit cards and room keys on board, is scanned. All bags go through x-ray, and smuggled alcohol is usually con-fiscated. It can be picked up at the end of the journey. A body search is routinely carried out if the metal detector goes off. This is impossible without female staff present.

Nike prefers to work with Israelis, men or women. They are tough, combat trained, and obedience is installed in them from birth. Young and fit. Ultimately it is make or break for them, since it's them or the Arabs. He has to admit that the grandchildren of Auschwitz survivors fascinate him. It is okay to say it out loud. Hitler is a popular first name in India. *Mein Kampf* was just reprinted in a classy new edition, and he has a copy on his bookshelf at home for everyone to see. So what?

A few years ago he went on a tour of Germany with his brother. They started in Herzogenaurach, to visit Puma and Adidas: business first. It was impressive how two global players emerged from healthy competition in this pictur-esque place. The Indians could take a page out of their play-book. Up the Rhine on a boat, and then a short visit to Berlin at the end, soil steeped in history. You could see immediately where the German determination comes from. They finish what they start, but Nike, who has been wearing Adidas ever since, thinks they persecuted the wrong people back then. That cannot be denied anymore. And, as already mentioned, he prefers to work with Israelis. The team that he got on really well with has been called back, from one day to the next. They are currently busy razing Gaza.

Miami took appropriate action. An internal paper was put together; the analysts crunched a bunch of numbers and came to the conclusion that there is such a thing as an ideal security team on board a cruise liner. Ideal in the sense of cost effectiveness and psychological profile: headed by an Indian with experience in the navy, police force, or hotel security; in the midfield, a couple of Gurkhas with front line experience, in case things get too dicey; and at the bottom, for patrols, the Burmese, who do not consider it beneath them to do deck work. The women are provided by the respective agencies, this one from Annapuma, in a three-pack with the two ex-soldiers, who do not ask any questions and obey him without question, despite his younger age.

Sure, he would prefer to have the men with him to face what is ahead, but now he needs people from whom he can demand complete obedience.

Deck 10. Nike pushes the button that prevents the doors from opening. Outside, there are a few children in their swimming gear. They will have to wait.

"Masarangi." Questioning eyes. Fear. That's good, that's where he wants her. He forces himself to speak quietly, almost tenderly. "I spoke to your boss before you came on duty."

It's impossible for her to mask her shock. "Dad?"

"I thought as much: your boss is your father."

Nike mentally pats himself on the back. Good, carry on. Just a hint. Her father would probably not be terribly pleased to hear that his daughter is involved with—well, with a trashy lounge singer, isn't that right? But don't you worry, girl. Nike will help you. He will help you find this singer. Just not now!

Now we have an emergency situation and that takes priority. "Understood, Masarangi?"

She nods. "Yes, sir."

There we go. Nike bestows a smile on the children outside the glass door and pushes the button.

Only the Frenchman is missing now.

Taking long strides, Nike drives the girl ahead of him down the corridor, past the officers' cabins. He punches in the number code. The door to the bridge opens. He nods to the Gurkha on guard duty and points to the right. The fruit arrangement on the coffee table is still under its cellophane.

The old man intercepts him, evidently in a hurry. "Come on, Mehta, let's go. We have to get out there and see how the people are doing. Women, children, pregnant women, injured?" Miami is putting pressure on the captain: when they will be moving again, the fuel costs. The Spanish coast guard is stalling him, can't get their asses moving.

The radio chirps. The captain has to answer.

Nike knows what to do. Where is the Frenchman? Ah, over there, in the ejection seat. "Officer Moret!" He cannot order him around, since his rank is higher. On the other hand... is this a threatening situation? Unclear. "Could you please?"

He comes over, and Nike pulls him aside, toward Masarangi. His orders are brief. "The three of us are heading out to the raft now." He and Masarangi will be armed, just in case. Moret speaks French, so he will communicate with the people if they cannot speak English. On board their lifeboat will be five water canisters, a first aid kit, blankets, and an injured person who urgently needs to get to a hospital. He slams the Syrian passport down on the table.

Nike ignores Masarangi; she won't complain. He turns to Moret and leans forward until their faces are separated by just a few centimeters. "Officer, we have illegals on board." For three months now. "And we both know why we have illegals on board. My people caught them at the breakfast buffet on the sea day between Malta and Barcelona. They were hungry." Gotcha, you rookie! Nike is not that easily deceived. "They remembered your unforgettable green eyes, officer."

He leans back and enjoys watching the man fold. It is the same feeling when you train, when your body obeys you like a machine and the guy on the bench next to you gives up, gasping for breath. Nike has complete control over his facial muscles. He listens to his inner rejoicing.

This arrogant young whelp, this coq au vin, he was long overdue.

CARTAGENA HARBOR | SPAIN

Diego Martínez

The light has that cutting clarity it always has when a storm approaches. Like large, dark birds, the old men are crouched in the midst of their massive pile of nets, as they patiently let the colorful webbing glide through their hands. No one looks up. No one says a word. The gulls circle overhead, warily eyeing their human competition, their cries filling the air, which smells of diesel and the stale fat from the kitchen at Club Nautico.

Diego inhales deeply the familiar scent from his childhood, as if striving to arm himself against the unpleasant things that are waiting for him. Remembers: on Sundays, if it had been a good week, the entire Martínez family went to the club. The women with shining hair, in their best dresses; the men in suits that fit increasingly poorly the older they grew. Somebody would always bring a guitar along. They ate fried seafood, they sang, and the children played, and when one of them fell into the harbor basin, one of the young men would pull his shirt off, flash his muscles, and jump in after him. Today, the club is frequented almost exclusively by yacht owners. They praise the simple, good food and the authentic atmosphere, according to Diego's brother. The fishermen wrinkle their noses. It hasn't been that good in a long time, and it is much too expensive for the likes of us.

He hesitantly sets off. His father insisted on sorting through the nets on his own, refusing to be driven home yet. Every week, he postpones the moment when they get into the car. His life is here. At home in his apartment, he is just an old man in everyone's way. He is so thin. Nobody would guess that they were father and son. Sometimes Diego is overcome with the desire to pick his father up, to show him how strong he has become. Instead, he lifts his hand in farewell. His father looks up, as if he has heard something, and nods.

Finally picking up his pace, Diego exits the fishing harbor through the wooden gate. Off to the right, the harbor road ends at a tall iron fence. He rings the bell and catches the eye of the security camera on the fence as it turns toward him. The gate swings open slowly, though not without a subdued rattling. He walks through, greeting the second camera mounted on a pole. In contrast to the fishing harbor, this harbor basin, the so-called Darsena de Talleres—the repair and assembly harbor—has nothing picturesque about it. The atmosphere is—how should he put it?—more functional. *Official* would be the wrong word, since there isn't enough activity for that. The sea rescue service and Guardia Civil share the offices on the second floor of the brick building that runs along the long side of the basin. Their workshops are on the ground floor, and in the back, at the end of the jetty, a semicircular window facade offers a view across the harbor. This is the command bridge of Cartagena's Salvamento Marítimo. Monitors, radar, radio. All news converges up there in the data center. Pale data crunchers, addicted to details, literally know everything about every ship in the harbor: how many thousand passengers are on the cruise ship that will arrive tomorrow; how many tons of corn headed for Ukraine are being loaded on to the German freighter sitting at the Santa Lucía wharf; which oligarchs own the superyacht that docked yesterday.

Contrary to his normal routine, he does not go straight to the staging room where he'll wait for the next deployment, the *Salvamar Rosa* berthed at her pier just outside. As always, it seems like she's telling him hello, a little shudder running through her garishly orange hull. Surely it is just his imagination, but you get used to such things. Diego would hardly be surprised if one day she whinnied like a horse, but today she will have to wait a bit longer until he can pay her some attention. Instead, he heads down the jetty toward the speedboats for the Guardia Civil. One has just returned, teenagers on board taking selfies. There is no mistaking the new agency director, out on a joyride with his kids. He's the one standing at the wheel, in uniform, with combed mustache and sunglasses, straddle-legged, chest puffed out.

Diego keeps walking. Talk about a showboat. It would never occur to the guy that he was misappropriating government funds whenever he took a police speedboat out for a private tour. Spain has people like him to thank for its crisis, though it is always others who end up taking the rap for it. Diego prefers to wear T-shirts with motifs from old sci-fi movies over tightly fitted shirts, prefers a full beard over a mustache. In his free time, he plays PlayStation, *FIFA* and *GTA*, why not? They all do it. He has respectable muscles from his work, but they conceal themselves behind the pleasure he takes from good food.

His mother cooks on Sundays; he cooks for himself during the week. He likes to experiment. There is no way he could still live with his parents and brother in that cramped apartment, stuffed full of memories from Escombreras. A combination of museum and day-care center. Every day, his sister drops the grandkids off before going to the Carrefour supermarket, where she works as a checker. Little Diego is hyperactive, pushing his grandparents to their limits.

All the firstborn sons in the family are named Diego. His father, too. If he ever happens to have a son someday, he will also be Diego. That is just the way it is for us, for the fishermen from Escombreras. They stoically call the neighborhood in Cartagena that the company built for them Escombreras. As if it could replace the original village. As if their obstinacy could prevent the village from being forgotten. However, the people from the city call their neighborhood Barrio Repsol. People remember the one who pays the bills.

Diego had been gone for a long time, traveling as a cook on the freighters. All the younger ones leave, moving far away for work, but as soon as they can, they come back and buy the apartments in which the old people have died. Diego took over his grandparents' apartment, when he started working for the sea rescue service. They do not want to lose their neighborhood to the newcomers. The Africans. The Arabs.

He is still walking along the jetty when his phone vibrates. He picks up immediately: the command bridge. What do they want? His shift runs for fourteen days and starts back up on Monday. For eight hours a day, they do maintenance work on the *Rosa* and humor her, so she is ready to thunder off like a racehorse at a moment's notice. For the remaining sixteen hours he is on call, which means sleeping with his phone, keeping his car close at hand, never taking his mother to the supermarket without having a plan B for how she can get her groceries back home by herself.

Today is his day off—they know that up there already. What don't they know? Can he fill in? His coworker is sitting at the dentist, root infection. The cruise liner is stuck twelve miles off the coast and is giving them hell because of a *patera*. They want to keep going, man. Can you go out?

Diego responds deliberately, as is his way. "We found a body while out fishing."

Yeah, they knew about that some time ago.

He has to go to the Red Cross, since the doctor and the Guardia Civil are waiting on him. He has to sign his statement.

"All right, my friend. But after that? Can you go? Will you come over, man? The *patrón* is all set to pull out."

The *patrón* is the jockey of the *Rosa*, a vain fellow who sports scrunchies that hold fewer and fewer thinning locks with each passing year. The *patrón* always wears a captain's uniform, which, strangely enough, comes with shorts that make him look like an aging schoolboy. Diego is much happier with his overalls, which match the color of the boat.

"What do you say, Diego?"

How can he say no, when there are people out there who need help? He can't. His brother will have to drive his father home.

"Good man, just hurry."

Diego enters the white barracks with its red cross that can be seen for miles around. This is the first stop for anyone they rescue from the water, whether shipwrecked sailors, stricken fishermen, or refugees. He walks up the steep stairs, taking two at a time. In the lobby, boxes of greeting kits are stacked up. One kit contains a pair of black shoes, like laborers wear. Blue overalls. A handkerchief. A bottle of water. The people he brings in are often wearing nothing more than damp rags. But the people the Guardia Civil take away all look alike. They are already wearing prison garb even before they land in the deportation cells.

Not that Diego has any idea what they should otherwise do with them. Time and time again, he has been touched by the euphoria that hangs over the *Rosa* after a rescue. It is truly contagious, especially when they thank him, hug him in their happiness. And then their exuberance evaporates like a puddle in the midday heat, once they grasp what is actually happening. He really has no idea. Should we let them all into the country? We are in the middle of a crisis, so we need each and every job. Should we send them on to the wealthy countries, the ones who have a say in Europe? Perhaps to Germany, to

Frau Merkel. That would serve her right. Good thing Diego isn't the one deciding. He has a soft heart and doesn't think he's a better person just because he is a Spaniard. He is proud that Cartagena has always been a Republican stronghold.

What are they talking about there behind the curtain? He will have to wait until they finish. It won't do any good to get on their case just because he wants to get out of here quickly.

He stares out the tiny, square barracks window at the fortress perched on the hill where the Gitanos live, on the other side of the road that leads to the hospital. Wherever you look, history is everywhere. It lies around where archaeologists unearthed it, but then they had no idea how to keep going once the crisis brought everything to a standstill. History piles on top of itself in Cartagena, literally. Way up there, diagonally behind him, is the Roman amphitheater, which was later used as a bullfighting arena. Now it, too, is collapsing and has to be shored up with red iron pillars. Phoenician, Roman, Spanish—nobody knows exactly what is going on. At first glance, it is hard to tell which houses are really houses and which are just facades. Half of the city center is nothing more than a stage set, held up by red pillars lined up against fire walls, insulated by ocher-colored foam.

We are trapped between the EU historic preservation regulations and the crisis. Whenever Diego thinks about it, he gets depressed. When he was little, Cartagena had still been alive: not a pretty city, but okay. A little disreputable even, the harbor quarter, lots of sailors, lots of soldiers. Today it sits under glass: halfway spruced up, harmless, lifeless.

Better to think about the Republicans. They fought here, made history here. During the First Spanish Republic, Cartagena was the most active canton among the federal states in the south. It even had its own currency: the duro cantonal. Antonio Galvéz Arce unfurled Spain's first red flag here, and the wild General Juan Contreras—yes, the same one whom

Diego, as a child, had sent out to help the Spanish troops against Lord Nelson—led raids along the Spanish coast in Cartagena's name. In early 1874, Arce and Contreras escaped the landward siege on a frigate, breaking through the sea blockade. The wind was blowing strong, and they sailed off, straight across to Oran.

The Second Spanish Republic. History repeated itself in 1939, during the civil war, right in front of this window, on top of those brown hills. Again the final battle was fought here. Again the Republicans had to flee across the sea, as Franco's Fascist troops approached from the land side. Again they escaped to Algeria. Or was it Tunisia? It is not quite proven but that is all right. At this moment in time, Diego's *abuelo*, his father's father, made his great entrance into world history. He was named Diego, of course, Diego Martínez.

"Diego Martínez?" The doctor steps out from behind the curtain, followed by a young policeman, who hands Diego the statement for signing. He writes out his name, the policeman vanishes again, all routine.

"I'd like to speak to you for a moment." A very young doctor, he introduces himself. His name sounds Arabic. He is wondering why the corpse has so many broken bones from just falling out of a raft.

Diego reiterates that all he did was find him caught in the net, as he had already explained in his statement. He had simply assumed he was an African from one of the *pateras*.

"Really?" the doctor asks, raising his eyebrows. "Assumed?"

Diego shakes his head. That is not how he meant it. They had not broken any of the boy's bones. The doctor keeps talking, growing excited. A body without a name, without a history, with serious injuries. He does not want to simply file him away like this.

Diego does not really listen. A memory keeps jangling in his consciousness. It takes a few seconds before he lets it in.

"A cruise ship," he hears himself say. "We've seen such injuries when someone has fallen from a *cruceiro*."

The doctor breaks off midsentence.

Diego exhales. He has to leave now, really. They have had an emergency call up there at the data center. Another raft. The people on it are still alive and need his help. Urgently.

The doctor is already turning on his heel and heading back behind the curtain. Diego hears him snap at the policeman for flirting with the nurse. Then Diego closes the door quietly behind him and hurries down the path to his next deployment.

AIRWAVES

Salvamento Marítimo: *Spirit of Europe*? Sea Rescue
                         Cartagena.

Spirit of Europe: Yes, sir, this is *Spirit of Europe*. I
                         read you loud and clear.

Salvamento Marítimo: Yes, sir, this is to inform you that
                         a speedboat is now proceeding to
                         your position, and we estimate
                         thirty minutes.

                    [Interference.]

Spirit of Europe: ....hirty minutes...
Salvamento Marítimo: ....hirty minutes to reach your
                         position.

Spirit of Europe: Okay, *Spirit of Europe* copy,
                         thirty minutes.

Salvamento Marítimo: Okay, that's correct, sir. Once the
                         speedboat arrives in the area, you
                         may resume your voyage. We will
                         be in contact, sir.

Spirit of Europe: Okay, thank you very much. *Spirit of Europe* standing by 27. Standing by for the speedboat.

Salvamento Marítimo: Stand by. Thank you.

SIOBHAN OF IRELAND | DECK A

Oleksij Lewtschenko

The sky is still blue, but the light is shifting. The horizon is too sharp.

Unreal.

Olek pauses and gazes through the diamond-shaped opening in the ship's wall, out across the open sea. Like a distorted window without glass. The *Siobhan* still holds surprises for him, even though he knows her architecture better than his own wife's body.

Irina. They've been married for twenty-one years now.

"What do *you* know?" she had snapped at him, when he'd been home the last time. Because he wanted to forbid his daughter from going to one of those demonstrations where the girls take off their clothes in protest. You want to rally against the invasion of Crimea? That's fine. But naked? Femen: founded in Kiev in 2008, the self-acclaimed feminist *grouhas* attracted international attention through their controversial demonstrations.

Changed. The Euromaidan protests have changed all of them. Mother and daughter drove to Kiev, and Olek had celebrated the Filipino Christmas with Dmitri and the crew in Oran Harbor.

His son spends the whole day in front of his PC, playing war. *Call of Duty*. The first-person shooter game puts the player in the role of an infantry soldier fighting in various World War II battles across Europe and Africa, while outside the real war is waging, right on our doorstep. It is time for the boy to go to the Odessa Maritime Academy. Perhaps he could make it as first officer, or even captain.

Olek descends a couple of steps. This is the spot where you can see the water rush under you.

Look away, quick. It draws you in.

Submerging.

Vanishing.

He turns to the left and forces himself into the narrow tunnel between the ship's side and the first row of containers.

He is safe here.

From whatever.

Why has he recently felt like he is always being watched? He can feel it at his back.

Anyone looking at you can see it.

It is damned tight through here, but he is used to it. Odessa is undercut by more than two thousand kilometers of catacombs—the old limestone mines; they even have secret passages to the open sea. Communist sailors once took refuge in the mines, as did the partisans later when the Germans besieged the city.

As a kid, Olek had played in the catacombs. They had fled, screaming, from the ghost who supposedly roams around down there. A woman, they say, who will show the way out to those who get lost, but they had not wanted to risk it.

He feels his way down the narrow gap between two containers. It's still there. The first row of cargo won't be unloaded until Castellón. The bottle is almost empty.

Takes a deep swig.

Holds the envelope up to the light. Official seal.

The mail rarely brings good news.

Another swig.

Olek stares at the container right in front of his nose. CMA CGM. Major global freight transportation company. Bigger and bigger ships, longer and longer, more and more containers. Explorer class, three identical ships with a holding capacity for sixteen thousand containers—the *Alexander von Humboldt* among them—photographed by Cosmochief during a storm on April 14, 2014, in Barcelona, five stars.

In comparison, the *Siobhan* is minuscule, steaming around and distributing what the large ones leave behind. The Mediterranean trade is dying. It is no secret that Collins is already accepting offers. Last week, he said that our good *Siobhan* is going to be sold to a Turkish shipowner and will soon be transporting steel from Ukraine to Istanbul, provided that Ukraine still has a harbor and Turkey is not overrun by one of those lunatics from Syria.

Shipping is a barometer for world politics. Even people like Olek, who are not the least bit interested in politics, hear about everything. Wars. Banking crises. Ebola. Fukushima. There's always a ship they know wherever anything is happening in the world.

Another swig.

Do it, don't be a coward. He studies the letter one more time from both sides. Neutral white envelope. A registered letter that Dmitri had to sign for with the harbormaster.

She wants a divorce.

Or his contract is not being extended.

But it doesn't matter; he can find a new wife or a new ship. Engineers are always in demand.

He tears open the letter resolutely.

Reads.

Drinks.

Reads again.

Turns the letter over, as if to check that it's real. It can't be true.

Olek starts to laugh. He sets the vodka bottle down, swallows the wrong way, has to cough.

Damned shitheads, what are they thinking?

He stops laughing and folds the letter up, carefully tucking it back into the envelope.

Oleksij Lewtschenko is being called up as a reservist in the Ukrainian army, effective immediately.

RAFT (NO NAME)

Karim Yacine

In order to not think about Zohra, he has to keep his thoughts here, in this boat, with these men who are about to die of heatstroke. They ran out of water a good while ago. Abdelmjid has stopped waving and is leaning back apathetically against the bulging rubber. He dipped his red cloth in the sea and has spread it over his face. Karim can't see his eyes.

Not good.

The five from the village have moved up to the front of the boat. The forced solidarity functions for a crossing, but not anymore. Nobody is looking over at the ship. Their gazes are turned toward the open water. One of them is mumbling something. Perhaps a prayer.

The teacher from Algiers has given the remaining cousin a pill. He is asleep now, his head on the older man's shoulder. The two boys from Karim's neighborhood are sitting in the middle, bent over the younger one's phone. The other one's battery is already shot.

The teacher is reading a book. A real book! As if he were sitting in a street café and not in a raft with no gas. Time and again, he readjusts his glasses, which keep slipping down because he is sweating so much. Karim tries to decipher the title. *Memoires d'Algérie*. The teacher glances up and hands him the book.

Karim studies it, turns it over. He has never really been a book person. College, his parents' dream for their children, shriveled up during the Black Decade. He searches for the name of the author. "A Jew wrote this book?" His voice sounds as mistrustful as he meant it to sound. Karim hands the book back.

The teacher removes his glasses and rubs them with the hem of his shirt. He speaks in a quiet voice. "A Jew who was born in Algeria and now teaches Algerian history in France. He collects letters and documents from the time of the war for independence and publishes them. Uncomfortable documents." He opens the book and extends it back toward Karim, who waves it away, pointing at the sun in the sky. Too hot. In reality, his French is no good. It is an uncomfortable reality for him. He should have learned more.

All these years in a holding pattern. The Black Decade. Darkness. Night. The Algerians have spread a blanket over this decade and all the subsequent ones. Spring does not come to Algeria. Not the Arab Spring or otherwise. Even when the government builds houses and awards microcredit. In Algeria, the generals reign supreme. The president is a sick, old man. Hardly anyone knows who is standing behind him: Is it the same men who prevented the Islamic Salvation Front from winning the elections in 1992? Their sons? Their grandsons? Do they now suddenly want to give up some of the wealth they extorted from the Algerian people? Nobody believes that.

In any case, Karim never received any credit, although he served his country.

He was fourteen years old in 1992, and early on, he sympathized with the Islamists. Why not?

Then his favorite singer was murdered on the street in broad daylight.

Then he was called up, at the age of nineteen.

"Better go." His parents were afraid for him, had been ever since one of his cousins disappeared into the torture prisons of the military police. Then a neighbor, a few weeks later, followed by the son of one of his father's customers. His parents shipped him off to the military because they were afraid for him.

Once there, he was told: "The Islamists will kill your families when they learn you're in the military." He was trapped.

He wore the black face mask of the Algerian Ninjas, so that nobody could recognize him.

He stayed, even after his military service ended.

It was 1997, and he didn't dare return home.

No one wanted the killing to stop. In the barracks, Karim lost the last of his illusions. Sometimes even they had no clue who committed the massacre last weekend. Fifty, ninety, two hundred dead. Clean up. Clear away. Cover.

Karim shot at least two men, perhaps more. He doesn't know.

Others, he has handed over. Were they all Islamicists? He doesn't know.

He no longer knows anything, not even if he had merely imagined hearing the voice of his school friend in the military prison, the one who had been a photographer.

No. *Is* a photographer, who lives in France. That is how Karim has pictured it. He has a wife and three children, and on the weekends, they go to the coast. He is doing well, his old friend.

He came down with shingles shortly after that, his entire torso full of it. The pain was unbearable, and they sent him back home. No sniper was waiting for him. Either they were all dead, or they had other things to do. Even today, he carries around a fear of that shot, just like the itch below his left shoulder.

The years following the war were restless ones. Karim hung around his neighborhood, always on the lookout for a good business proposition. He tried his hand as a taxi driver, then a mountain guide, but very few tourists came to Algeria. After 9/11, even that had dried up.

The time of the Harraga began a little after that. The Algerian teenagers take off in rafts, and Karim was one of them. It was like an addiction. He tried it again. And again. Getting better and better, wanting to outsmart the Spanish coast guard at all costs. And made it through.

He made it for six months last time. Then they caught him on the TGV, on his way from Paris to Zohra in Marseille.

Zohra.

Merde.

After his deportation, he had applied for the microcredit to start a small transport company that would run from Oran through the Sahara. If he wants Zohra to return, he has to offer her something. She needs good doctors, a car. Karim's brother was approved for the credit, but his application was rejected. He made a down payment on a property up in the mountains, with a view across the plateau to the sea. He drove up there every day, afraid that the owner would find another buyer who could shell out the whole sum. In his imagination, he built a house in which he would live with Zohra. At some point, it was finished, and he could describe it in great detail, as if it really existed. Come in, may I introduce you to my wife? Here is the living room. And over there, the kitchen. A conservatory here, because sometimes it gets really cold up here and Zohra can't stand the cold.

Zohra.

Stop it, Karim.

He would like to ask the teacher what he is searching for in Europe, if he has a family. It would force him to stop thinking about Zohra, but before he gets around to that, the teacher suddenly jumps up and points over at the ship. The rubber raft lurches, and Karim throws himself against the edge, equalizing the boat at the last minute with his weight. Abdelmjid grabs the handkerchief from his face.

"Man, they're lowering a boat down!"

"Finally!"

"I told you they would!"

All of a sudden, all of them are wide-awake.

Karim doesn't say a word.

He watches the boat slowly glide down the side of the ship. There are people in it, though he cannot tell how many. But he sees how the tourists are all bunching back together again. He notices the flash of their camera lenses in the sun. As the rescue craft touches the surface of the water, he hears a noise. It sounds like the flapping of a sail. He squints to see better, and then he realizes what they are doing.

The people are clapping.

They are huddled together up there on the decks, clapping.

As if this here were *Alhan Wa Chabab*, Algeria's *American Idol*.

CARTAGENA | SPAIN

Zohra Hamadi

These figures on the wall make her dizzy. Slapped on with simple black strokes, the mute silhouettes stare out to sea, just like she is. And yet they each seem to be moving, rising up like a vortex from the shadow of the harbor jetty, at the end of which a red lighthouse rises.

Zohra looks away, at the water, then back again, at the graffiti. There is something comforting about the vortex people. She cannot explain it, but they are also waiting, and she feels less alone. She leans against the warm wall and closes her eyes for a moment, becoming one of them.

The call was short, much too short for his words.

"We are stuck here without fuel, somewhere off of Cartagena. I set you free."

I set you free, as if one could simply return a heart that was given as a gift. Karim will go to prison, possibly for many years, but damn him, he should have asked her at least. He should have asked her and looked into her eyes while doing so. Anger rises from her stomach and claws up her spine. The pain follows like an echo shortly afterward, filling her entire body.

Breathe, Zohra.

She breathes.

In the first moment, down there on the beach, she thought it would kill her. The anger, the pain, the loneliness. Her expression must have frightened the blond child, since it ran back to its parents. Zohra could feel their gaze from under the parasol.

A woman, alone.

A woman with a headscarf, alone.

A woman with a headscarf, alone, and a child who runs away.

The collective shock pierced her like a sound wave. She turned and began the long walk back to the car. She drove on, as if in trance, until the tears and back pain made her stop. She had reached a town.

Cartagena. So close to Karim, and yet beyond reach. She walked as close as she could toward the sea and ended up here, at the wall, with the mute shadows. The waiting ones.

At home, in Marseille, Zohra rarely wears the hijab, only when she feels insecure, exposed to strangers' glances, like now. It is a deeply rooted tradition, inherited from her *maman* and she from hers. Nobody forced her. Zohra's father is the director of an elementary school near Sidi Bel Abbès. He cannot stand the bearded ones. "They destroyed the Algeria your grandfathers fought for," he always says. An independent, secular Algeria.

Zohra's mother urges him to speak more quietly. "It is dangerous, Djamel, what if someone hears you? You know." She bites her lip. Father breaks off. Everyone is quiet; the only sound is the scraping of their knives and forks on the plates. Everyone knows. Everyone knows what can happen if someone hears or sees.

On a Saturday in September 1997, Zohra was fourteen; the sky darkened shortly after three. Rain in September was almost unheard of, and yet it was raining when the minibus, with eleven of her father's colleagues in it, encountered a roadblock. Eleven female teachers, who had been warned anonymously that:

Western education is haram.

Women who work are haram.

Students who do not wear the veil are haram.

They had refused to stay at home, and Zohra's father had supported them in this. He thought it was right for them to resist intimidation. The Islamists pulled the eleven teachers out of the bus and slit their throats, one after the other.

"Even the sky cried," the people say.

Year after year, along with the teachers' relatives, Zohra's family attends the memorial service held on the twenty-seventh of September. Year after year, her father's hair grows whiter, his gait more stooped. It never leaves him, the monstrosity of these murders, which lost significance in the midst of the horror that never seems to end in these days. Not a day goes by when there is no murder, when one does not hear of someone going missing, being tortured or kidnapped.

Years later, the man who gave the order for the teachers to be murdered was arrested. He came from the same village in which the school is located. He is the father of three daughters. He is a shepherd.

Years later, her father still writes a memorial obituary for the local paper every autumn.

Years later, Maman whispers: "Go to France, my butterfly, go to your brother."

Before it starts again. No one says it, but many think it as they watch the evening news. The Islamists have a strong following, in Iraq, in Syria. And behind closed doors, some do not think it is such a bad thing. We should not put up with all this.

Zohra opens her eyes and is back at the harbor wall, the lighthouse in front of her. At the pier across from the entrance lie two large gray warships. Even in the sunshine they look threatening. She shivers and shifts her gaze farther to the right.

Come.

Here.

Karim.

No sense waiting. No sense driving on. He didn't even give her enough time to tell him where she is.

Zohra is angry. Her back aches, and her future is crumbling. The sea and the sky meet in a sharp line of blue. There is a fortress on the other side of the bay, built into the mountain. An old fortress, and above it, radio masts and satellite dishes stretch upward. The whole city is like this, an old city, Cartagena. She recalls that her parents most likely had been here once, maybe even right here: a pleasant thought that comforts her.

Before Zohra was born, Algerians were permitted to vacation in Europe, just like everyone else. After their wedding, her parents got on an airplane and flew half an hour from Oran to Alicante, just like that. They lay on the beach in Benidorm for a week, at her mother's request. And then a week-long tour, to please the husband, who cannot get enough of all things old. The slides are brought out time and again, whenever someone in the family has a birthday or when the fast is broken.

A radiantly orange ship approaches the harbor exit. Zohra has déjà vu. I have seen it all before, this ship, this orange, this blue sea. In a moment, it will be parallel to her, just one of the many silhouettes against the harbor wall. It has to pass quite closely. Zohra watches a plump figure on the prow of the ship in orange-colored overalls, head under a white helmet, like an astronaut in a film.

Film.

Video.

Karim's video. The Harraga on the lifeboat, laughing, high-fiving. Rescued. The boat, the bright color.

Focus, Zohra, what did Karim say on the phone? Their fuel had run out. They were waiting for the Spaniards to come and save them.

The Spaniards. He explained it all to you, back then, when he proudly showed you the video. The blue circle with the yellow anchor is the symbol of the sea rescue service. It is always better when they come and not the Guardia Civil, although it doesn't make a big difference. You are treated better, but you still end up in the deportation prison.

Before she can second-guess herself, she has raised her arms and waves. "Stop!" She plunges forward, out from the shadow of the wall. A strong gust of wind hits her back and pushes her over the sloping edge toward the water, as the pain returns. She flails helplessly with her arms in the air. The man with the helmet looks over to her at the exact moment she loses her balance.

Fate.

Ten minutes later, she is sitting in the back of the boat with a blanket around her shoulders. He crouches before her, tidily winding up the cord of the life belt. He has taken off his helmet.

They are speaking English, although neither of them really can. He always looks over that way, he says, because his grandfather was thrown into the sea there.

He fell into the sea?

"No," he says, "my grandfather's ashes."

Zohra sees the pain in his eyes and nods. "I'm sorry."

"It's all right," he says. "My *abuelo* was very old."

Abuelo?

Another man in uniform joins them. Zohra pulls the blanket around her body more tightly, wishing she could hide in it. They speak Spanish, quickly and harshly. The boat moves away from the harbor jetty.

"I'm sorry," says the one who saved her. "We can't bring you ashore now. We have to head out. Emergency." He points out. *"Patera!"*

Zohra does not immediately understand. *"Zodiac?"*

"Yes, yes!" He nods. *"Zodiac."*

She smiles. "All right. No problem."

No problem.

He puts on his helmet and disappears up front again. She snuggles into the blanket and unwinds her wet headscarf, so her hair can dry in the wind as the sun warms her face. The pain has slipped away. From afar, the black figures look like real people, slowly disappearing into the white spray the boat is creating. Zohra waves to them. You keep on waiting. I am going to Karim.

She reaches for her bag to get out her phone.

Call Karim.

But the bag is not there. She must have lost it when she fell in the water.

Car key. Telephone.

All gone.

LIFEBOAT IV | *SPIRIT OF EUROPE*

Lalita Masarangi

For a brief moment, she imagines it is Jo, there on the stretcher, after the rescue. She has the sheet lifted, and he's looking at her. *Titanic* flashback: the two of them at the prow, his body pressed to hers, his breath on her neck.

Hey, come on, pull yourself together, girl.

The man under the sheet is in a lot of pain. He's groaning. She can only guess his face under the cloth. Instead, she peers at Nike, who is radioing with the bridge. Léon is actually the superior officer here, but in security situations it is different, says Nike. And Léon does not argue, does everything he is told. Fetch the water canisters. Do this, do that.

Something is not right here.

Since their brief conversation on the bridge, Nike has taken complete control. He is vibrating with energy, evidently enjoying the whole thing, like the way he had Deck 4 sealed off around the lifeboat, chop-chop. The way he steered the wheeled stretcher toward the lifeboat with one hand, as if it were empty. Nobody noticed anything. He had even posed for the tourists' cameras, his guru smile at the ready. Spooky.

Oh well, Lalita got what she wanted. Once the poor guy here is on his way to the hospital, then they will search the entire ship for Jo. Why they aren't calling a helicopter or handing the injured man over directly to the sea rescue service, she has no idea. She doesn't want to know even as Nike directs them to take the stretcher onto the lifeboat.

Jo.

Please let him be alive. Maybe a broken leg, lying somewhere, unable to get up by himself. But nothing terrible.

Nike shoots her and Léon a sharp glance and nods. Léon starts the engine, and the lifeboat starts moving. She feels tiny right up against the ship, as if someone had reconfigured them to their correct proportions. Back on deck, the sea looks like a harmless blue surface, a carpet over which they float. Down here, it seems cold and voracious. They move away quickly, as the people applaud.

Just take a look at yourselves.

She had heard it, somewhere on Deck 12. "Why do we have to wait for someone to pick up the garbage over there?"

"It's their own fault."

"Let them snuff it."

"A few more or less."

Drivel, drivel.

And the others, the know-it-alls: "Shouldn't we send them straight back?"

Should we? Could we?

"Mama, what are the people in the boat doing there?"—"They're going for a little dip, sweetie. You can see that."

An image comes to her mind. Why now, no idea. Aldershot, two old Gurkhas with wizened faces sitting on a bench in the empty shopping mall, quietly engrossed in conversation. They are taking a walk down memory lane. This campaign, that attack. Right next to the bench is a group of Teletubbies waiting for children to set them moving. The colorful figures are covered in a layer of dust in which someone has drawn whorls.

Aldershot is a real double lie. Brits complain all the time about the little grannies, who walk behind their athletic men in traditional dress. Who pee in the parks. Who know nothing about British culture.

Thing is, apart from them, no other fuckers ever come here. Take a look around you! The city has three empty shopping malls. The army is cutting back; it doesn't give a rip about you.

If it wasn't for us, who else would send their children to your schools, would fork over your taxes, pay horrendous rents for your dilapidated houses? And who would protect you from the terrorists you fear so much?

The security people at the 2012 Olympics were Gurkhas.

All of them, down to the last man.

The second lie is carried to Europe from Nepal in a suitcase. The little grannies hide their homesickness under their knitted caps. Their men march through the drizzle every day for kilometers on end in order to not grow rusty. They are stubborn old warriors whose eyes beg to be accepted as equals among equals. They convince themselves that things are better in England: better doctors, better medicine. It will be easier here as they grow older. And then it is the yearning that kills them.

Lalita remembers a story that her grandmother once told her, when the summer lightning behind Annapuma had been so bright that she couldn't sleep.

"What's behind the mountain?" she wanted to know. And behind that? And behind that?

Grandmother had heard the story from her father when he'd come back from the Great War.

One day, when they had stopped counting the days in the Half Moon Camp, Great-Grandfather was brought into a barracks where men were gathered around a funnel, German men in fine suits. They dragged him over to the funnel. One of them, who spoke English, demanded he say something in his language, anything, into the funnel. Behind the funnel was a machine, on which a disc turned.

Great-Grandfather was frightened. A Gurkha is made to fight, he thought. If only he had his dagger, then he would send them all packing, the machine as well.

But he had no a dagger, so he told them how it was:

Hear ye, hear ye. Now hear:
We came on British orders.
Three streams of water in a village in Nepal.
Water running, endlessly.
We are not dying, but even alive we are not living.
The soul screams.
Hear ye, hear ye. Now hear what I have to say to you.
Like bubbling water
My emotions bubble inside me.
Is it possible to appease these emotions?
Hear ye, hear ye. Now hear what I have to say to you...

Lalita balks. What came next? Forgotten. Shit. But she remembers the end.

My body is hot, cool it with a fan.
I don't want to stay in Europe,
Please bring me back to Nepal.
Gurkhas eat goats, but not swans.
Survival is not progress,
Death does not bring knowledge,
I understand nothing.
I tell God that my journey is long.
That is why I want to go back to my village.
I want to leave this country.

He later said that he had hoped they would kill him for these words, but they had just nodded, clapping him on the shoulder and switching the machine on to play. Great-Grandfather heard his own voice. They were delighted, took the disc made of wax and went away. They had stolen Great-Grandfather's voice. Many years later, one of the few things that he left behind was the piece of paper carrying his speech from the camp in Germany.

"So don't ask what lies behind the mountain, little Lalita. For in the end, you might lose your pretty, cheeky voice. And now go to sleep." Grandmother switched off the light, and the summer lightning was over.

The man under the sheet is tossing and turning back and forth, mumbling words in a language Lalita cannot understand. She gently strokes the place on the sheet where she thinks his head is.

Who are you? Where is your home? Who are your parents? Feel, I am here. Everything will be all right.

Listen closely.

I will tell you a story.

RAFT (NO NAME)

Marwan Fakhouri

Where am I?

Where is she? The voice. Goats, but not swans.

Concentrate, Marwan. Brain hemorrhage. You should be operating now. Marwan should operate on himself. His hysteria rises. Not possible. A fit of laughter shakes him, and he feels tears shoot into his eyes.

"Calm down, man. Calm down."

Arabic. Someone is speaking Arabic.

Marwan grins. Am I back in Aleppo? Did I not run away? Can I take back the decision? It was the wrong one, do you understand?

Stop.

Back.

Back to the last night, to the break between two operations, a cigarette among friends, their faces gray with exhaustion. Can you hear me, friends? We have to hang on, regardless of how desperate the situation is. Maybe there is no more hope for Syria, but we have to carry on, do you understand?

"We have to carry on!"

Blue. Water. Sun. Tartus. Harbor town on the Mediterranean. Marwan's home. Russian warships bob by the pier. His father is a petrochemical engineer. The gas deposits in the Levant Basin are unimaginably large, boy.

For hours on end.

Yes, Father.

Don't you understand, son? They want to prevent us from becoming the new hub for gas deliveries to Europe.

Who are "they," Father?

The Emir of Qatar, the Turks, the Iraqis, the Sunnites.

And who are "we," Father?

We back Assad, son. We are Syria. We have powerful allies: Iran, Russia. We will defeat them.

We, Father, we are no longer Syria. Not me. Assad bombs his own people with rockets, Father. I stitch students back together, Father. Students who were attending peaceful demonstrations, Father. Barrel bombs on the hospital. It's not just propaganda, Father.

The pain pulses in his brain like liquid lava. Don't get agitated. I mustn't get agitated. The patient must remain calm. We don't have enough medication.

Blue sea. Sun. Silent images. Family trip to Arwad. White boat. Fortress on the island. Resting in the shade. Blue T-shirt, white trousers. Big agave. Restaurant in the harbor. Blue-and-white plastic tablecloths. Sunday. Super 8.

I am not in Arwad.

The smell of rubber baking in the sun.

I am in a rubber raft, on the way from Alexandria to Italy. Always goes on Thursdays. First the money, then off we go. The big fishing boat stops in the middle of the ocean for the transfer to the raft.

Far too many people. "Here's a cell phone. Call the coast guard in Malta. They'll fetch you."

Dial tone. No reply. Dial tone.

Far too many people in the raft. Hunger. Thirst. Dial tone.

"Over there! Look, guys, a cruise ship!"

Marwan makes the effort to lift his head. There we go, now he can see.

Up, up high. Right up to the sky.

Stop.

Why is the sun shining? It is nighttime on the raft off the coast of Malta. The *Spirit of Europe* is taking us on board. Euphoria. Sandwiches. Marwan and Oke.

No, no, it is all wrong. The sun should not be here.

Switch off the sun!

Super 8. Wrong film.

Sybille Malinowski

"No!"

It is dark. Sybille is standing on the wharf. They are now hauling up the gangway. The ship gleams in all its splendor, as huge as a castle, its lights sparkling. It is frosty, and her hands tingle. Hands, feet. She spends hours every day telling herself that her hands and feet are still there. "If they fall off, you'll notice it!" Wiltrud giggles. She has red cheeks, much too red. It is the frost.

She is standing on the wharf, stamping her feet against the cold and in anger. She wants to get on. Wants. Must. The anger is warming her up through and through. She is ten.

"I'm cold!" her little sister whines. "You said that we'd go on that ship and that it'd be cozy and warm there."

"Shut up!" She sees the tears flow and regrets her words instantly. "We'll take the next ship." She already sounds like their mother.

"No no no!" Wiltrud shakes her head, her tears flying.

Father had promised. He had promised that he would come. We have to wait.

There are people up there at the railing, black silhouettes against the bright glare. They wave, and laughter floats down to them. She has never wanted anything as much as this ship. Dear God, fix it so we can travel on the *Gustloff*.

A couple of years ago: every few months, Tante Hilda came from Leipzig, bringing books and presents with her. She was stunningly attractive, sporting the latest fashions from the city. We could never get enough of her, our eyes devouring every detail. She always brought clothes for Mother and sweets for us. She read magazines, and one of them showed a photo full of women clad in swimsuits, sun worshippers on the upper deck of the *Gustloff*, traveling to Scandinavia. The magazine stayed behind, but Tante Hilde left and never came back. Instead, the war came.

For once, do what I ask, most beloved, finest Father in Heaven. Please! She stamps her foot one more time. The ship's horn sounds.

And the boat departs.

The next morning, all three of them are standing in the harbor. Wiltrud clutches Mother's hand and hurls deadly glares at her from behind the woman's back.

They both caught a slap this morning. Mother had swept into the room and yanked them out of bed. Then they all screamed at one another simultaneously. As far as they could understand, Mother had waited up half the night, before nodding off in the armchair. This was why she had not heard them when they slipped in.

She does not comprehend the excitement. It's all right, Mother! They didn't take us along. They didn't let let us on board, Mother!

They head over to the parsonage, where the naval chaplain has been able to scrounge up three tickets for the *Hansa*. "Go, madam. Go in the name of the Lord and take your daughters to safety." Sybille hears the fear in his voice, its shrillness. "You will not make it any farther on foot. Foot travel has been banned, as the soldiers are flooding back in.

Twenty kilometers, madam, the Russians are only twenty kilometers away!"

The icy northeast wind blows straight out of Russia. The Baltic is leaden gray. They are standing on the wharf, which is rapidly filling up as the people reassemble. The chaplain promised to bring their things with a wagon.

They are waiting. They are always waiting. Where is Father?

The *Hansa* is moored over to the left. An entirely normal ship, dull.

She feels like she does after a night of fever, as her teeth chatter and her knees threaten to buckle. But her body wishes to heal, wishes to see springtime, the buds, the wild geese in the sky. Wishes to feel summer, the warm sand under her toes; wishes to stretch out in the grass and listen as the lark rises on its song into the sky.

She gazes up.

Is that a wild goose crying? A single, much too early wild goose? Has it flown off course?

The city is behind her, and she can feel in her spine the eerie tension that has settled over it.

Excited voices around her. "What—what are they saying? Mother?" Mother just shakes her head. "But I heard, Mother!"

The *Gustloff* was sunk last night.

Corpses are drifting in the gray Baltic. Hundreds. Thousands.

It is cold.

Sybille awakes after the sun has disappeared. She keeps nodding off; it must have something to do with the medications. The doctor says they just need to make the fine adjustments, figure out the right dosages for the Parkinson's, which could take a long time. In his roundabout way, he means it could draw out for years. Sybille knows all about this, having been a specialized orthopedics sales representative. She had worked a lot with Parkinson's patients.

These will be years in which nothing will get better, years in which her world will become increasingly small, increasingly limited.

Store the horizon, Sybille. Draw this boundless sky into yourself. Save it. You'll need it.

A fierce wind drives heavy clouds toward them, and suddenly, the sun breaks back through again, way out there, transforming the sea into a dramatic play of colors, of black, white, and silver. Ah, how lovely.

Her thoughts soar, across the sea, then across a different, Nordic sea. She is a lark, singing and rejoicing. She feels the beginning of her swooping arc, the power of each individual beat of her wings. She sees, far down below, herself and her two children playing in the sand. She sees herself as a young girl in a sailboat. She flies on, across the sea. Sees herself standing that morning on the wharf, next to her mother with Wiltrud by the hand. Somewhere behind them is the house of her childhood. Somewhere behind them, their father is leading the horses into the barn. They never saw him again, their father. His trail lost itself in Russia, and she cannot follow him.

Nor can she follow Tante Hilde, or her husband, the newspaper publisher. Leipzig once had a large Jewish community. The children were taken to safety with the help of German friends, but the parents were lost. Somewhere along the way to Auschwitz?

Sybille's father refused to believe this. Something like this could not happen in Germany. Her mother said nothing.

Lines from a poem suddenly spring to Sybille's mind, something that's only recently started happening to her. Memories ascend like bubbles, torn completely out of their context.

Did you close the door softly
For the last time
As you left
Fearful
Tearful
Frightened
Lonely without us
Gone long ago...

Max had sent this to her from England, many years later, after they had found each other again. These were the parting words from a Jewish poet to her mother. The guilt of having survived, which the boy, her cousin Max, never got over.

The correspondence between Sybille and Max began like a tentative caress and has lasted forty years. She can no longer write, so she has to be grateful whenever someone types a few lines out for her on the computer, ones she has freely formulated from her mind. That, too, will not last much longer.

Her thoughts tremble, like her hands.

What is that? Applause?

Sybille emerges fully from the world of her thoughts, though her mind balks. What could it possibly want in the here and now of pain and helplessness? In astonishment, she realizes that she is surrounded by empty loungers.

Whatever it is must be going on on the other side. What are they clapping about? Have they finally rescued the poor people from that awful raft? Always this unhealthy fixation on the spectacle. A new sensation has to be cooked up every five minutes.

The music is already blaring again.

And Wiltrud is gambling somewhere. My little sister.

Sybille and her husband used to read a lot, as a means to cope with the war and their own history. She is always startled by the lust in her peers' faces, the greed. Ambition may be a virtue, but at what point does it cross the line? Lust for food. Lust for life. Lust for careers. She can see the greed in Wiltrud's eyes, when she claims she is just going to take one more turn out on the deck to stretch her legs.

If she thinks about it objectively, it has always been complicated between them. Wiltrud constantly strove to get the better of her: she went on to finish high school, then college. There was no point in discussing anything else. Later it was a Hamburg shipper's son, who had more family wealth than Ulrich could ever earn as the head physician at a hospital. Already early on, Wiltrud's children learned how to elude her demands. And now it is obviously the addiction to the lucky strike. The money means nothing to her, since she has enough already.

Sybille is frightened that Wiltrud will not be able to find her, even if in a moment of clarity she does recall that her sister is all by herself on deck, dependent on her help. The girl from security surely forgot about her long ago.

Has a cruise passenger ever died of starvation or dehydration? Fat chance. The idea of starving in the midst of this abundance actually makes her laugh.

Pull yourself together, Sybille. You have to do something, right now, before you are too weak because you failed to take your pills. It is now or never.

She reaches behind her. The wheelchair is there. Step one, step two, step three. Everything in due order.

She shifts her center of gravity so that the footrest sinks.

Her torso comes upright, as her head flops onto her chest. Now she can only look down.

She grabs her left leg with both hands and sets her foot on the floor.

Now for the right leg.

Foot on the floor. Pay attention! Don't tip to the right.

Centimeter by centimeter, she scoots her body ninety degrees to the left. Stands up.

The wheelchair has to be to the left of her, so she waves blindly in that general direction until she hits something: the armrest. The wheelchair is sitting with the seat toward her, the brakes on.

No chance.

She must spin around. Hand back again. Holding tight with both hands, her feet scuttle to the left.

One, two, three. Forward, millimeter by millimeter.

Done.

Now grab the armrests with both hands.

Hold tight.

And pull.

One, two, three.

Get up, you old nag.

Done.

She releases the brake. Now she can use the wheelchair turned backward as a walker.

She has to follow her instinct. The casino is in the ship's stern, to the right and down, so to the elevator.

Good luck. She cannot see what is in front of her, just the floor. The floor is light yellow. Watch out, an edge. Now red, dark red.

The blow comes hard and without warning.

She staggers and uses all her strength to lift her head.

She is standing on the jogging track!

The young man is already gone, and all she can see is his colorful outfit, earphones in his ears, muscular calves.

She can no longer hold her head up.

Something pops in her back, directly below her neck.

Second, third, or fourth vertebra.

Osteoporosis. Porous. The vertebrae are cracking, and the doctors have advised surgery and infusions with cement, in order to stiffen the vertebrae.

She feels dizzy.

I'm scared.

Suddenly hands. Hands and voices. Someone grabs her, twirls her around, and pulls. Don't pull!

She falls back into the chair. Red floor. She cannot see the person. Hello, I don't see you. Who are you?

In her ear. English. "Madam, your cabin?"

"Casino," she manages with effort. "My sister is in the casino. Wiltrud Herrendorf."

Dark red. White stripes. Light yellow. Green.

Where am I?

Panic.

"Let go of me! Get my sister! Right now!"

The wild ride ends instantaneously.

"As you wish, madam."

Green. Fake green grass. Yuck, how tasteless.

She is cold. She would like to go to the cabin, take her pills, slip under the warm cover, sleep, dream. Her eyes are already closing.

"Sybille!" All she can see are Wiltrud's legs, slender in white cropped pants. Brown ankles, sandals, painted toenails. "I told you to wait for me!" She doesn't need to look up to see what kind of look Wiltrud is now throwing her. Deadly, like back then in Gdingen.

All your fault.

The legs crouch down. She smells of alcohol, as something tumbles out of her pants pocket. A silver chip. She steps on it. Too late, dear Wiltrud.

Forced cordiality. "I'll take you to the cabin now, okay?"

Sybille lifts her hand.

Swinging door. Elevator. FRIDAY is written on the foot mat. Today is Friday.

Corridor. Patterned rug in brown and yellow.

Cabin. Rug. Pale green.

Humming. Safe. Open. Shut.

My jewelry. The code is our mother's birthday. Wiltrud keeps her chips in there. I cannot get to it anyway. My hands tremble. I cannot hit the buttons or even stand.

Sybille would like to sleep.

Her fourth thoracic vertebra has collapsed.

Nikhil Mehta

Smile!

"Please, officer, look this way!"

Very well. He straightens up, shoulders back, stomach in.

"The uniform suits you, officer!"

"Thank you, ma'am." They press their sweaty bodies against his. The men get all chummy and sling their arms around his shoulders.

Smile!

Right, that's enough now.

Soon he won't have to wear this ridiculous *Love Boat* uniform anymore, that's for sure. His lawyer's email should be arriving any day now, and then the path is clear. Back to India, right to the top. No one to stop him.

NaMo—that's what they call him in Gujarat—has been prime minister of India for over a month now. Our man Narendra Modi is like a one-man task force: a tsu-NaMo after his overwhelming election victory. May he bring India as far as he did Nike's home state, Gujarat. It was an economic miracle in the prosperous north, nothing short of that. The Indian middle classes need growth, prosperity, and security. It has all been just talk for too long. The Nehrus and the Gandhis have clouded our minds. Jai Ram!

I tell it like it is. Since the terror attacks in Mumbai, we once again know where the enemy is located. In this regard,

I sympathize with the colleagues from Israel. The world has reached a historic watershed, if you know what I mean. We have to make a decision, and India has decided. We *are* the twenty-first century.

Nike steps back from the people and watches as the Burmese remove the barrier tape. The show is over. He is happy with the way things turned out. There is always a solution, and Miami will see it that way, too.

Done. And now on to the jobs at hand. In his head, Nike runs through his to-do list.

Report. The first officer has already gone back up to the bridge, but he is not part of the chain of command for security issues. That's between Nike and the captain.

Then Miami. A video chat with Sheila is probably in the cards.

The Nigerian will have to stay for the time being. As long as he doesn't cause any trouble, that's fine with him. They must find a political solution, sooner or later. He'd prefer later. He will talk to the man himself.

Masarangi should set up the conference call now. Where is she anyway? Ah, over there by the door, waiting for his orders. He sends her down to the office.

He turns and is halfway up the stairs before she materializes next to him.

"Sir!"

"Now what?"

"You promised—the singer. What are we going to do?"

What are we going to do? "Girl, he hasn't even been missing for twenty-four hours. Not even his band has raised the alarm. As long as they don't complain, it's not my responsibility."

Where are we? Deck 6. He pulls her into the Maharaja Lounge, where everything is decorated Oriental style, the way Americans like to imagine India, including fake elephant and tiger heads on the wall. The Filipinos are running through their program as usual, with the guy on bass doing the singing. They don't even need the singer. Note to self: Email the cruise director a memo. Save on costs.

The early drinkers are seated in front of their cocktails. Bad weather means cash.

"I want to hear it from them, all right, girl? You go over there now and tell them that if something isn't right, then they should come straight to me. Got it?"

She nods and walks across the lounge to the stage, where she waits until the number is over.

You can't let talk like this become a habit. At some point, everyone starts unloading on you. It's in situations like this that true management skills reveal themselves—leadership. God knows Nike has completed enough of these seminars in the last few years. Miami is crazy about them.

Never mind that he had learned everything there was to know about leadership as a boy in the RSS. Its opponents call the Rashtriya Swayamsevak Sangh the cadre factory of Hindutva. Yes, and we take it as a compliment!

NaMo and Nike's father were there close to the same time—in different *shakhas*, the local groups, but they knew each other by sight. Nike and his brother also joined as soon as they were old enough. The greatest thing for him was the annual summer camp, the Sangh Shiksha Varga in Gujarat. That feeling of exercising with thousands of comrades: morning training, cricket, yoga. Physical discipline is the name of the game: RSS's credo since its founding in 1925. Sure, it was around the same time as the Hitler Youth! The model isn't exactly a secret. But we still exist, and we have achieved everything: the end of British colonial rule in India, the national reconstruction of the Indian nation as a Hindu cultural entity. We even supply the prime minister. What more do you want?

His phone rings. The bridge reports that one of the suites is asking for Officer Masarangi from security. They put her on. The passenger is a woman, elderly by the sound of her voice. Nike can barely understand her; her English has a strong German accent.

"Ma'am, how may I help you?" He makes sure to keep the right amount of respect in his voice. The Germans are his favorite guests, but not only because of the sneakers and Hitler. They stick to the rules. The only thing that bothers him is that they keep calling security about the towels left on the unoccupied sun loungers. She mumbles something about her jewelry and asks that the woman be sent up. "Masarangi. Yes, she'll be right there, ma'am."

Even better, this way he'll be rid of her. Nike makes a mental note of the suite number. Indian students have to memorize so many things, so a four-digit number is child's play for him.

The band has just stopped playing. Polite applause. He watches Masarangi talking to the bass player—Raymond is his name, isn't it? Raymond laughs and waves her off. Masarangi's mouth twists. She should be careful; making sulky faces like that will give her wrinkles sooner than she likes.

She comes back. "They say he's always skiving off." She doesn't buy it.

Nike takes her arm and guides her toward the staircase. "Look, girl." The fatherly approach. "You're getting all worked up, officer. Let me explain something to you. On average, five thousand people live on this boat. Most of them don't know each other, and yet there are rarely any accidents or crimes on cruise ships. Isn't that astonishing? Of course, there are exceptions, but we aren't going on that assumption yet. We're assuming that your singer is somewhere on board, sleeping off his hangover. If that isn't the case, then he's no longer on board. And I'll tell you now..." He lowers his voice.

They are on Deck 7 now, just where he wants her. The library is in the bow, and like usual, it is completely empty. The only person in sight is a boy lounging on one of the artificial leather seats, playing with his Game Boy. Nike motions for Masarangi to join him between the dark wooden shelves, fake veneer that looks like warm tropical wood. "If he's no longer on board, then there's a ninety-nine percent chance that we're dealing with a suicide." Her eyes widen with shock. "Yes, Masarangi, face up to the facts. Only the strong survive. And the weak..." Well, how should he put it? "A cruise ship like this seems to be a magnet for such people. They come on board as crew members, and when the moment comes, they jump. Sometimes it's bad news from home that's the last straw. Or a passenger who woke up on the wrong side of the bed. And you know what, Masarangi? Not one of those wastes a single thought on the problems he causes us, you and me. We have to inform the rescue service, which, of course, can never find a person on the high seas without exact coordinates. No chance. Then the paperwork. The harbor police. Miami. Worst-case scenario, the whole story appears on one of those cruise haters' blogs, and the family of the victim initiates years of lawsuits, from one case to the next. My worst nightmare. Your father's nightmare. And yours in the future. Do you often have nightmares, Masarangi?"

She shakes her head.

"Good. Consider yourself lucky. I have them." He lays his hand on her shoulder and points to the left. "Now off you go to Suite 7945. The lady specifically asked for you. And I'll take care of your Jo, if it becomes necessary."

She disappears without any further objections. That turned out to be easier than expected. I will take care of it. Nike the Fixer.

He storms up the next flight of stairs. As soon as he's done with this job, all the illegals and suicides, the greedy, the sick, the gambling addicts, and the sunburn victims can all go to hell. But until then, he needs to keep his nose clean. They screen you very thoroughly in the president's Special Protection Group. Even NaMo can't do anything about that, though it has been hinted at to Nike that there would be a position for him there. As long as he can get an acquittal in that old matter and if his files are otherwise clean. These files happen to be in Miami.

He takes the last flight two steps at a time. It's just a couple of meters down the hallway to the bridge.

He will go in there now and report to the old man. The people on the raft: only men, no women, no children, all in good health. They distributed ten liters of water and blankets, and informed the men that the rescue service is on its way.

"No further incidents, Captain. All under control."

Followed by a video conference with Miami.

Followed by a conference call with Annapuma Security. Masarangi Senior, once a soldier, always a soldier. He will get his daughter under control.

Nike punches in the code on the keypad, and the door to the bridge opens. He nods to the Gurkha who is still standing guard.

The old man is pacing up and down; everyone else is standing around, waiting. Moret is seated in front of a computer, poring over some maps. Navigation. Weather data. If the captain weren't here, they would be betting on which would get here first: the Spanish sea rescue service or the storm.

"Finally!" The captain, too, wants to get back to his office, seeking coffee and God knows what else. A sleeping schedule too irregular for too long. Many people take pills against that. He is restless, like a tiger in a cage. "Mehta, where have you been all this time?"

"Emergency on Deck 7, Suite 7945." Cover his back. "Either burglary or dementia."

The old guy laughs, and Kiyan, the second in command, grins. "Good work out there, Mehta. As far as I could see from up here, all clean and according to regulations."

Nike delivers his report as planned, the way the captain wants to hear it.

The radio crackles. Moret swivels around, leaps up, and covers the distance to the microphone with long strides. A quick glance at Nike.

Wait a second, did Moret just smirk a little? Nike is alarmed.

"Anything else, Mehta?" The captain yawns.

"No, sir."

As if prearranged, both of them look toward Moret, who is fumbling around with the buttons on the radio set without looking up.

"Gentlemen, I will be downstairs. We will get moving once we have the go-ahead from Cartagena." The old man motions for Nike to leave the bridge with him.

Not that, please, despite his love for Germany. Captain Björn-Helmut Krüger is famous for his never-ending monologues on world events. A staunch Social Democrat. In India, he would be a member of the Congress Party.

Such men are anachronisms, history.

Today is NaMo.

Tomorrow is Nikhil Mehta, alias Nike the Fixer.

AIRWAVES

Spirit of Europe:	*Spirit of Europe*, go ahead, please.
Salvamento Marítimo:	This is Sea Rescue Cartagena. You want information about the speedboat? ETA... [incomprehensible] in fifteen minutes. Ten to fifteen minutes.
Spirit of Europe:	Okay. ETA to our vessel is ten to fifteen minutes. Thank you, Sea Rescue Cartagena.
Salvamento Marítimo:	Yes, when the speedboat arrives, you can proceed on your voyage.
Spirit of Europe:	Okay. *Spirit of Europe* copy. When the speedboat is here, we can proceed with our voyage. ETA ten to fifteen minutes. Thank you. *Spirit of Europe* standing by 27.
Salvamento Marítimo:	Okay, thank you very much *Spirit of Europe* for your cooperation.

SPIRIT OF EUROPE | BRIDGE

Léon Moret

Ha! Things will get going in a moment. Léon rubs his hands together, stretches and switches off the radio. The *Salvamar Rosa* will be arriving from approximately north by northwest. The quartermaster is already in the ejection seat.

"Visual contact?"

"Not yet, sir."

But Kiyan has already spotted the speedboat on the radar and is transmitting the position, about three more nautical miles to go.

The timing is perfect. Léon had anticipated that the captain would have gone back down again by now, but the fact that Mehta, the snake, is also gone—it could not have gone any better. Léon steps up to the panorama window. The ejection seat has the port side in view, so he strolls over to the bow just to take a look. Right at the end of the bridge, the windows wrap around, commanding a good view to the side and the back. Far out, the damaged raft is bobbing up and down. It is already drizzling. The arrival of the storm couldn't be better timed.

He stands up very close to the window and whispers: *"Bonne chance."*

The wind picks up, and concern flickers up for a moment: What if they capsize in the storm out there? Rubbish, the guy he talked to was as calm as they come, keeping a straight face as he explained that there was gas in the last canister. It was a good thing that Nike and the security chick don't speak French.

Léon turns and walks briskly back to Kiyan, who is still following the *Rosa* on the radar. The raft is too small for his antennae, which is why they cross the Mediterranean on these air mattresses. Léon glances over Kiyan's shoulder and then goes to the control desk.

Suddenly he trips over a barely perceptible edge in the thick blue velour. He just manages to break his fall, catching himself on the desk.

The foghorn.

The mighty sound propels the quartermaster from his seat. Kiyan rushes out from behind the curtain.

"Oops." Léon straightens up. "That was close."

Kiyan casts him a scrutinizing glance. Careful, that one is not so easily deceived.

"Officer Huang!" Léon bellows a little louder than necessary. Kiyan snaps to attention. "Make a log entry: At"—he makes a point of looking at his watch—"seven minutes past three CET, an unintentional activation of the foghorn by first officer on duty, Léon Moret, in order to avoid a workplace accident. Report that to the captain."

Léon blinks slowly and yawns. He doesn't need to pretend to anyone that he is completely exhausted.

"Five minutes, max," Kiyan says with a smile. "I'll wake you up."

He's already lying on the sofa, eyes closed. If he stays cool, then the others will, too. Then nobody will pace up and down and possibly notice that the raft has disappeared. Kiyan is already talking quietly on the phone in the background.

It had been a spontaneous decision, because Mehta had annoyed him so much. Then the shock of finding out that he knew everything. The feeling of "What the hell?" had set in immediately afterward, followed by: "There's no way you're going to put up with this."

Honestly, who does he think he is? Does he think he can call all the shots? I mean, I haven't made a single mistake on duty or anything like that. I'm an outstanding navigator, finished top of my class, and sailing, as the captain calls it, is in my blood.

I was able to sail before I could even walk. When I surf, I'm like the cresting wave itself, and when I kitesurf, I can always catch the wind with my chute, because I can see it. Not really, of course, but in my head, with my inner eye. Georges, my father, says it's as if I had a sixth sense for the sea. It scares him, because he is a scientist. For him there is no God and no magic, just intellect. If you don't use your intellect, then you only have yourself to blame, he says.

Georges. I don't call him Papa, because somehow he is not a typical father. Not bad or anything, just different. Sylvie, my mother, is more of a *maman*. At least she used to be.

"You got your pigheadedness from you father, Léon," Sylvie insists. She sometimes utters this reproachfully, whenever he runs off again. Always down to the harbor, always onto the water. Sometimes she says this proudly: *You're not easily fooled.* Sometimes sadly: *You don't even ask me, Léon. You just do it.*

Shit, I have to send them an email again. How long has it been since we saw each other? Almost a year? I just can't make it work. On board, you forget that there is a world out there that keeps on turning, one in which Georges from the Île d'Aix drives to the factory every day to fiddle around with his rare earths. He occasionally pops in at the University of La Rochelle in the afternoons to hold a seminar at the Laboratory for Environmental Sciences. This is the world in which, with every passing day, he postpones the moment of homecoming to the certified organic cocoon, where now only

Sylvie and Fabian live, without Léon, who, let's be honest, did a runner.

Fabian is twenty-eight and works in a workshop for the disabled on the island. Sylvie takes him in the mornings and picks him up again in the afternoons. In between, she sorts out all the other stuff; running an eco household takes a lot of time and patience. She has her vegetable garden behind the house, the old farmhouse that they converted themselves, bit by bit. It is not even five hundred meters from the beach. A wind generator is located in the yard, since there is always wind on the island. The solar collectors are up on the roof. As a family, we're genuinely off the grid, and not just since the time it's been possible to buy solar panels in the hardware store.

Léon remembers how the people called his parents freaks even when he was still at the island school. Georges in particular was not popular—a taciturn, bullheaded guy who only opened up when his favorite subjects were discussed: environmental destruction, protecting nature, and so on. He was not one to while away the time in the bar with the fishermen. An oddball. A know-it-all. An ecological stiff. That doesn't go down well when you're eight years old and your brother is the spaz.

Nobody on the island knows why Georges moved here with his family. People assume that the Île d'Aix attracts folks like this because cars are prohibited here. However, Georges is on the run, if what the boy Léon heard every couple of years was true, whenever Georges indulged in a glass of red wine and was not just mutely brooding over numbers at his desk. At first, he would sit in front of a gridded notepad, later a computer. His back, which the three of them got very used to seeing, remained the same.

"You're a paranoid nutcase!" Léon shouted at his back many years later, before he left the house, never to return.

"If you say so, consumerist-crazy asshole," Georges replied, without turning around.

It's a badass story, though Léon doesn't care whether it's actually as shocking as Georges claims. The fact is that Georges was once a perfectly normal young geologist who, after finishing college, went straight to the French multinational Peñarroya, because it happened to be looking for geologists. It sent him and his wife to a mining area in Andalusia. Georges was happy with his work, got on well with the Spanish miners, and moved into a small house right on the coast, in an old fishing village. The giant hotels and holiday resorts didn't exist on the Costa Blanca back then. Sylvie planted her first garden and grew vegetables like all the other women in the village, then Fabian was born. It was a shock for both Georges and Sylvie, because Fabian was the way he was. Special.

"Your brother is special, Léon, not a spaz. Remember that once and for all."

Léon loves Fabian; no one should get the wrong idea. He would kill anyone who wanted to hurt Fabian, because his brother is like a special stone.

Léon and Georges used to pore over their quartz collection for hours on end. "Why is this one expensive and this one isn't?"

"Because it's rare."

"But the other is much shinier when you hold it against the sun."

Fabian is also shiny. At first, they didn't notice anything, only that he was difficult and always crying. Then they realized that something was not right, and then the rafts arrived.

Sylvie claims that was the day that Georges became the Georges we know today. Three rafts from the *Sirius*, the first official action by Greenpeace Spain, in August 1986. They stood in front of the pipes in their protective suits and let the filthy sludge cover their bodies, making a visible statement for everyone who hadn't gotten it yet. The filthy sludge was being washed out to sea from the ore being cleaned in the Lavadero Roberto treatment site. The images traveled around the world.

After that, Georges began to take soil samples and discovered that the lead content of the soil in the village in which they lived was over twenty times higher than the permitted peak value for men, not to mention pregnant women. He found other substances, right on the beach, where they swam on Sundays.

Arsenic. Sulfur. A Pandora's box of horrors.

Georges left Sylvie and Fabian with the grandparents and sued his own company, ruining himself in the legal proceedings. The mine was eventually closed anyway, because its yields dropped. He was encouraged to resign but refused. The company was sold, broken up, given new names. Georges received a proper notice of dismissal, but the lawsuits continued until he lost control of his car one day on the way back to the village and narrowly missed a deep ravine. He insisted that someone took a shot at his tires, but the police declared it an accident.

The three thousand families in the vicinity of the mine who lost their jobs blamed either Greenpeace or the crazy geologist.

Georges vanished in the middle of the night, collected Sylvie and Fabian and moved to the Île d'Aix with them, near where the University of La Rochelle was introducing the master's program in *sciences pour l'environnement*. Sylvie wanted a second child, so Léon was born. Léon, the beach child with eyes as green as the Atlantic.

Léon's first lesson was: "Look around, what do you see, boy?"

"I see the beach and the sea, Georges."

"Yes, Léon? And what else do you see?"

"Nothing, Georges."

"Look closely. It looks like the beach and the sea, but death may be lurking in there, Léon. Don't trust anyone who tells you that it's only a beach by the sea. And now we're going home to Sylvie and Fabian."

Léon opens his eyes and grins. No wonder he has a sixth sense for the sea. Cover all the bases. Don't trust anyone.

Good old Georges. Rebel.

He never wanted to be like his father, so obstinate and unhappy. Not a coot. Not a crank. But of course, something had stuck: this extreme sense of justice. That is why he filled the canister with gas. That is why he whispered to the guy on the boat: "Wait for my signal, then scram. And take him to a hospital." The Syrian.

All because Mehta treats people like pawns. First the stowaway with the head injury, then the people in the boat. In the end, they will all be put on the next flight home, and it will all be for nothing, while Mehta rubs his hands with glee and slips off the hook again.

Léon should have let the captain in on it, back then when he realized that the two party crashers had disappeared and Mehta had mistakenly sent too few people off the ship. At the latest, he should have said something today, just now, before the Indian completed his report.

But he hadn't, because he wants to keep his life here. So he found another way to set things right.

"There they are!" Kiyan has caught sight of the *Salvamar Rosa*, which will be within range in ten seconds. "Nine, eight, seven. Up you go, Moret!"

Léon is immediately awake. Another occupational hazard.

He reaches the window in three strides. The sky is dark gray now, and a flash of lightning lights up the helipad on the bow.

There is the *Salvamar Rosa*, all in orange, as it drops into a wave trough.

Léon wishes the men in the *zodiac* luck.

I hope you make it.

There is thunder outside.

Why is this song going through his head now?

Despite all my rage
I am still just a rat in a cage...

Seamus Clarke

"Sláinte na bhfear!" he bellows over to the men in the raft. Take care! A half-turn on one leg. Uh-oh, don't lose your balance. Seamus raises his Guinness: *"Agus go maire na mná go deo!"*

Yes, may the women live forever. Now down the hatch.

That's good stuff. It's a pity that Kelly is playing bingo, because, first and foremost, that wish goes for you, my luv. To our daughters and their daughters, and all the women of Ireland.

Ha! Not a soul out here on deck, all because it's blowing a little. Where are all you twats? Did the rain drive the fine gents indoors?

It was cozy in the pub, yes, it was. He'd retreated to his regular table, up there in the dark corner, from where he could keep them all in view, all those people strolling along the promenade deck and shopping like there was no tomorrow. Kelly had gone to bingo, which is sooner a woman's thing. The pub is not really her thing either, all the crush and the sweat, although there's never much going on around midafternoon. The British gents don't drink until five, and the ones from the Continent only after eight. So you can always tell the Irishman right away. Seamus was standing at the table with a pint in hand. And then this guy walked by, a tall blond fellow. He caught sight of him only out of the corner of his eye, and again he thought: Kevin.

That's how you'd look, Kevin. That's how you'd look today, if you were fifty like me. We'd be standing here together, drinking our pints, and our wives would be together upstairs at bingo, Kevin. My Kelly and your... Mary? Admit it, you were crazy about her. Three years older than us, Mary was the queen of the soapboxes and not afraid of anything, not of the street corner below or of the bloody Brits.

Kevin.

You know, Kevin, my throat's parched. I'll get us another pint. I've got this, man.

Seamus had gone to the bar, where the barkeeper was already filling the next Guinness.

I'm back again. *Sláinte,* Kevin. Cheers. Those boys out there, those boys in the boat, they remind me of us. We imagined we'd run away together to New York and join the Irish Mafia. We'd become rich gangsters or something like that. It's so bloody gray in Belfast when you're thirteen, Kevin. Remember that? We were already in the midst of the war back then, marching in the lines of the Fianna Éireann at ten. Remember they called us the IRA's youth organization? But actually we were just the kids from Turf Lodge, from Falls, from all over West Belfast, who'd had enough of having to get out of the way of British tanks when walking home from school. Who'd had enough of constantly missing someone at supper because he'd been arrested. Who'd had enough of waking up every morning to the deflated feeling that there'd be bad news on the radio today. You know what, Kevin? I still listen to the news every morning. And each time my heart jumps a little when I pour my coffee and switch on the Grundig radio. Yep, it still works, the old box. German quality, made in Belfast. The manager back then was abducted by the IRA, and they shut the factory down. My father, Chris Clarke, had worked there, but you know that anyway.

Kevin.

Do you still recall how my dad used to run around with that tape recorder? I don't know if he started doing that when the Troubles started or before then. Maybe he bought that portable recorder cheap from Grundig. I got my collecting bug from him, you could say. Nothing could keep him at home after work or on the weekends: he was always out on the streets. He'd walk around the area for hours, making recordings. Short chats with the neighbors about this or that. Explosions. The screams from the barricades. People running. Breathless accounts from eyewitnesses. I've got piles of tapes in my cellar. My brothers think the family archive should stay together, and I'm the keeper of this historical collection.

Do you think I've listened to them even once? Honestly, Kevin, I don't have the guts. Dad and Mum are both dead; he went first, then she a few years later. He was a strange man, my dad. It bothered him: the killing, the dying, the rage around us. I also got that from him.

But I wanted to tell you something else. On that day— you already know, the one you— Well, my dad had gone back out again. I was about to leave, and then he came back.

"No way," my dad said. "You're not going out. Too dangerous."

"But I have to—"

Nothing doing. I briefly considered simply slipping out anyway, but then he looked at me that way, as if he could read my thoughts. "Go upstairs."

So I went up, then looked out the attic window.

And I saw you waiting for me on the corner, Kevin.

And I wonder today: What would have happened if my dad had come home two minutes later? Would I have run across to you? Would we both be here today? Would I have died, and would you be here instead of me?

I've always felt guilty. At first, I was furious, so much so I wanted to join up right away, but they wouldn't take me. I was too young, they said. Then almost to the day, two years after your death, I was arrested. They came to our house.

Bam! Bam! Hammering on the door. My dad was out again, so my sister opened the door. Deirdre, she later married and moved to Toronto. The cops asked for Seamus. Actually, I'm pretty sure that they were after Rob, but either someone had given them the wrong name by mistake or they simply mixed us up. Anyway, before I could bolt, they were hauling me out. I was only fifteen, but they still took me up to Castlereagh, into the lion's den.

Three days of interrogations. I didn't say anything, only that I wanted to join the IRA, but they wouldn't take me. The verdict: two years of house arrest. Had to be sitting at home every day by six P.M. "Don't you dare show your face outside, boy."

All I could do was watch everything from the attic window. Do you understand, Kevin? That opening wasn't even a square meter. My life forced into that square meter. I was fed up, Kevin. I was young; I wanted to dance, listen to music, ride a motorcycle. I was nineteen, Kevin, when I got married. Now I'm fifty and a grandpa twice over. That's how it is.

I need some fresh air. Will you come out with me?

That's how he landed all by himself out there on the deck. Yup, a fresh breeze always does wonders. The foghorn blows. Holy Mother of God, that's enough to burst your eardrums.

Did I do the right thing, Kevin? Or am I a wretched coward? I don't know, but perhaps you do. Yes, you out there in the raft, the one with the red cloth.

Kevin!

Seamus sets his empty beer glass close to the door. A really nice swell. Deck 4 rises and falls, rises and falls. The first raindrops lose themselves among the lifeboats suspended over the railing.

Nevertheless, Seamus pulls his video camera out of his pocket and takes off the lens cap: routine gestures done umpteen times, familiar.

Seamus films.

Wait a sec, am I seeing things? Is the raft moving, or is it just the wind? Aye, they're clearing out. I've got to be crazy.

Seamus lowers the camera and squints into the misty gray. It thunders. The machines beneath him hum.

Who's moving? They or we?

We're moving.

It looks like a storm's coming.

"To your health, men, arrive safely. To your health, Kevin. May the Holy Mother of God protect you."

Long live the bloody *Titanic*. Head held high, straight to its sinking. The *Titanic* was launched from Belfast, and now they've built an entire museum for it. For a damned ship that sank with man and mouse on board. How morbid is that? How can we live in a city that has produced nothing but death and doom?

Tonight is Formal Night. I'll lead my lady dressed up to the nines to dinner, and they'll be astonished. We're Irish, and we love any excuse for a good knees-up. Come rain or shine.

Seamus throws one final glance at the rough sea. Deck 4 is now completely desolate. Water is spreading out across the floor, turning it into a reflective surface.

The automatic door hisses open, and inside, the Filipino combo is fighting its way through this week's charts more pathetically than usual.

Seamus decides to lie down for a short nap.

SALVAMAR ROSA

Diego Martínez

The storm front is coming straight at them from the north, with the boulders of Cabo de Palos vanishing from one moment to the next. Gusts sweep over the leaden-gray sea with gale-force winds of eight, nine. He stands on the bow as the first breaker arrives, and the *Rosa* begins to buck like a furious horse.

Downward.

His eyes scan every square meter of water in sight, and he lets his thoughts run free.

It was March 5, 1938, when Commander Luis González Ubieta sailed out here on the bow of the *Libertad*, leading the Republican fleet from Cartagena to Palma de Mallorca. Actually it was late evening, but that doesn't matter. You could barely see your hand in front of your eyes. The two cruisers and five destroyers were navigating with darkened lights. Their goal was to infiltrate Palma Harbor and to stage a surprise attack against the Nationalists there. Suddenly González Ubieta noticed dark silhouettes very close by: ships, large ones. The two fleets were circling each other in the dark. Neither fired a shot, neither wanted to make itself a target by opening fire. In the end, it was the Fascists who lost their nerve first.

Thoughts speed back to the present. They must be drifting somewhere! Hell is about to break loose here. Diego leans out with his whole weight between the *Rosa*'s metal bars.

There's nothing to be seen.

The *Spirit of Europe* is rapidly departing. They want to reach Mallorca yet tonight. It's no fun in this weather, with all those vomiting tourists on board. Diego would actually really like to take a cruise sometime with his entire family. Well, maybe later, when he has the money for it, when the times are better, when he actually has his own family. Maybe.

The radio blares in his ears. The *patrón* is bellowing at Cartagena for sending the *cruceiro* away too soon, and now we can't find the goddamned raft.

Where's the helicopter?

Alicante. Too far away, but it should come anyway.

"Can you see anything?" That's for him. Diego knocks against the outside of his helmet. The damned headset has a loose contact. He lifts his hand, thumb down. Negative.

You'd think it would be easy. The wide sea. A single boat. You couldn't miss it. But these *pateras* are like gelatin. They wobble between the waves, too small for the radar to catch.

The *patrón* flips on the searchlight.

Up there! Is that it? He wipes his eyes with his sleeve.

An illusion.

The wind tugs at his overalls, and he turns around. The girl is standing behind him. Oh God, he'd forgotten all about her. She has pulled the cover around her shoulders and is gesturing. Girl, you'll fly away! He places a hand on her shoulder, and with his other, he pushes her slowly but steadily toward the cabin. He can hardly get the door open, as spray drenches the back of his overalls.

Finally inside. The *patrón* is still on the radio. Diego gestures that she should sit down: a bench, a table, no luxury, but better than nothing.

He points to the Thermos: "Hot coffee!"

She wants to say something, but he has to get back out.

"I have to be out there. You understand?"

She nods.

Back out. At first, the noise is deafening. The storm has arrived. It thunders. He struggles, step by step, back up front to the lookout.

Nothing.

Even if they find them, how is he supposed to get them on board in this surf? That's the critical moment. One false move, one guy too frantic, too excited, and the rubber boat will tip over. Those things are way too unstable, and once the people are in the water, most of them can't swim. They drown before your eyes, and you can't do a thing. Nothing worse.

Spain's worst ship catastrophe.

He had just been thinking about that.

His *abuelo* mentioned it only once. The day on which he had watched 1,476 men drown in the sea before his very eyes. Diego was still a boy, so that had to have been in the late eighties. Franco was finally gone, and his grandfather had received a medal and had needed a brandy. His *abuelo*, like all the men in the Martínez family, was no great talker, but on that day, he had talked, while the whole family listened. The children sat breathlessly under the table, hoping that nobody remembered them and sent them to bed. Diego would later play the scene out over and over again with his Playmobil figures.

March 7, 1939, one year after the Battle of Cabo de Palos, shortly before the end of the Spanish Civil War. Catalonia had already fallen into the hands of Franco's forces. Only Cartagena was left, barely held by the Republicans, when the uprising broke out here. The Fascists had already declared themselves the victors, and they sent their fleet from the north in order to occupy Cartagena. The Republican ships were fleeing across the Mediterranean, but the Republicans quelled the uprising with their last remaining resources, regaining control of the powerful guns on the fortress around Cartagena. One after the other, Franco's ships turned around. Only the *Castillo de Olite* kept going. She was navigating blind, without radio contact, the only ship in the fleet that passed Isla de Escombreras, and the soldiers assumed that the other ships had already taken the harbor. They sang Nationalist songs and unfurled their flag. A shot thundered from the cannon above Escombreras, grazing the ship.

The songs fell silent.

The second shot went astray, and then panic broke out on deck.

The third shot was a direct hit on the munitions depot. As the *Castillo de Olite* broke apart, men, or parts of them, flew high into the air, right before the eyes of the fishermen from Escombreras.

Diego Martínez and the other fishermen didn't waste much time, before they ran to their boats and headed out. Over the course of one night, they pulled hundreds of injured, shivering men out of the cold water. Many of them were killed by their own comrades as they tried to climb over one another into the tiny fishing boats.

Afterward, they hauled the dead ashore.

The Republicans took the survivors off their hands and carried them away, grumbling about the fishermen who felt obliged to rescue Fascists.

The war ended twenty-five days later, General Franco the celebrated victor.

A couple of weeks later, soldiers returned to the village, this time Franco's Guardia Civil. They were looking for the cashbox from the sunken *Olite*. The wife of the lighthouse keeper, an ardent Fascist, sent them to the fishermen. The soldiers seized all the men in the village and stuck them in prison, but the cashbox was never found.

That's how it was back then. The fishermen had to pay for the fact that they had saved lives.

"And you know what, boy?" His *abuelo* had pulled little Diego out from under the table. He had peed in his pants in excitement, but the old man didn't care. "I would do it again. Do you know why?" Diego didn't. "We, the fishermen from Escombreras, won't let anyone dictate to us what is right and what is wrong!"

It thunders. Diego's gaze wanders involuntarily toward the coast, over to where the old cannons are still standing on the summit. But the coast has disappeared behind a wall of rain. There is nothing to see, just water, everywhere.

No raft.

He feels helpless. Weak. Powerless.

First the dead boy, and now the raft is gone. We always arrive too late. The Mediterranean is filling up with bodies, like a mass grave, and we continue to go swimming on the weekends at the beaches of El Portús and Portmán.

Pull yourself together, Diego Martínez.

"There's no point. The helicopter should keep searching." The *patrón*'s voice rattles in his ears.

Diego lets go of the bars. He now notices that, despite his gloves, his hands are very stiff. That is how hard he has been holding on.

He lurches toward the back and throws himself against the door.

And is inside.

The *patrón*, Jorge is his name, has his hands full keeping the *Rosa* on course. Diego removes his helmet, his hands shaking. He desperately needs a cup of coffee. The passage down below is so narrow that he can hardly fit through in his overalls.

The woman is leaning against the cabin wall and has shut her eyes. Diego sits down quietly beside her and pours himself some coffee. He squints to the left, not wanting to stare at her. Maybe she really is asleep. She's pretty, but not as young as he'd thought. A wrinkle on her forehead. She moves, and the wrinkle deepens as if she is in pain.

At least I pulled you from the water alive, beautiful. How did you land on the harbor wall at Cartagena? Why did you want to plunge into the water? Or did you slip?

He wants to know. He rescued her, so her life was in his hands. He feels a need to protect this life, as if it is especially valuable, especially fragile. One life against so many deaths. That is his deal with the devil on this day.

She moans in her sleep, as the wrinkle deepens even more. He looks over very shortly, then back away, before taking a sip of coffee. Very slowly, like in slow motion, he begins to feel the rolling of the ship under him. Then the girl's body as it presses against his, slumping until her head rests on his shoulder.

Don't move.

We'll just sit like this.

Forever.

Lalita Masarangi

Outside the suite's panorama window, the weather's reminding her of *2012*, that apocalypse movie. For a moment, Lalita forgets why she is here, then the woman in the wheelchair clears her throat. "We don't have much time. My sister might return any minute."

Thunder rolls.

"Yes, of course. So sorry, ma'am. What can I do for you?" Lalita feels like her head might explode. This day never seems to end. She is still on duty, still has no idea where Jo might be.

"Are you still looking for the singer?"

Lalita nods. Is that why the old woman asked her to come? Doesn't she have anything else to do?

She moves into the light so she can get a better look at Mrs. Malinowski. *Better* is the wrong word, since she is now looking right down at her head. The silver hair falls in silky, thin strands from the side part over her ears. She wasn't this stooped before. I can't see her eyes. Creepy.

"Ma'am, you reported a burglary? Please tell me what you are missing, and since when." Stick to protocol, security training. Stay objective. Don't get drawn into personal conversations. Attentive but noncommittal. The passenger is always right. Fulfilling a dream. Western Mediterranean.

My head. Nightmare.

"I fear something has happened." The old woman speaks downward, as if to herself. She cannot raise her head, but why not? Why do people get so bent? Lalita would like to straighten her up.

What is that supposed to mean? "Ma'am, I'm sorry, I don't understand—"

"Come with me." She shuffles forward, moving the wheelchair across the suite, centimeter by centimeter.

Lalita shuffles forward alongside her and feels stupid.

"Open the safe."

Now what? Is this a trap? The others tell stories, in the evenings in the crew bar, about passengers who make a joke out of framing crew members for some offense. They quite calmly watch you being fired and disembarking in the next harbor, just for the fun of it. How sick is that?

"Open it. I'll give you the code."

And then? Then I'll be standing in front of the open safe, and the sister will show up and find me alone with this helpless old woman. Lalita shakes her head. "We're not allowed—"

Mrs. Malinowski interrupts her. Her wheezing sounds like the very loud rustling of leaves, like when you shuffle your feet through autumn foliage. "Good God, girl, you can see that I can't reach it!"

"Please calm down! Please." All right. If she insists. She goes to the safe and waits for the woman behind her to give her the four-digit code.

The safe springs open, and Lalita sees jewelry boxes, old-fashioned ones, made of blue and red velvet. Next to them, neatly piled by color, sit a large number of chips from the casino.

And in front of them piles... Oh no.

She picks it up: a silver triangle, rounded at the edges, a hole through it, engraved with a jumping dolphin. The Dolphins at Dawn.

His guitar pick. He wears it on a silver chain around his neck and takes it off only when he plays the guitar. His lucky charm.

How did it get here? In this suite? With the German woman?

"Can you remember whether he was wearing it last night?"

Of course she can remember. Of course he was wearing it. He never took it off. It was a gift from Bella, his grandmother. Bella, the freedom fighter. *You remind me of her, Gurkha Girl.* Lalita turns around, the plectrum in hand, and crouches down. She has to see the face.

The eyes squint up at her, behind the gold-rimmed glasses. "I'm afraid my sister may have had something to do with your boyfriend's disappearance." She makes a helpless gesture with her hands.

Lalita takes the hands in hers. They are ice cold. "Can we ask your sister?"

Mrs. Malinowski shakes her head. Resolutely. Okay, so no. Is she frightened of her sister? She is probably dependent on her, but Lalita has to know what happened. She is sure now that something is not right, since he would never willingly take the guitar pick off.

"Shall I report it?" The head shaking again. Yes, no, it's pointless. No evidence. And Nike wants absolutely no more trouble.

Okay.

The casino. "Your sister plays in the casino regularly?" Nodding. And Jo worked there, at least according to the bass player. Was the sister there last night?

She doesn't know. Her medication is too strong, and she sleeps like a log.

Lalita suggests they check the CCTV cameras again. There are more than a thousand cameras on board; one of them must have recorded something.

Mrs. Malinowski is horrified. This surveillance is terrible. What about privacy?

Lalita pushes her across the corridor to the elevator. "It's for your own safety, ma'am."

The woman has forgotten her pills, so that means back to the suite again and then back to the elevator. Wait. "Are there some here, too? Everywhere? Are we being monitored right now?"

Lalita has to laugh. "Don't think of it like that. It's not as if there are twenty people sitting and watching what's going on in every little corner of the ship around the clock. We can activate the cameras by hand. A maximum of four at the same time. The data is stored, and people feel safer."

"Not me." She feels watched, controlled. She grew up in a system like that. Everyone was monitored; nobody could escape. "You are naive, young lady."

Of course she's naive. This is getting better by the minute. Her boyfriend has disappeared, this woman's sister had something to do with it, and she is naive.

The elevator stops, and she pushes Mrs. Malinowski out onto Broadway.

It's better if not too many people see her, since Broadway is strictly off-limits for passengers. No exceptions. They have no business here. This is no place for dream vacationers.

Then again, Lalita is security, and security is allowed to do whatever it likes.

"Oh, gray linoleum," she rustles from below in the wheelchair.

"Don't speak, please." She should damn well keep her trap shut. "Keep your feet up." Lalita picks up the pace. The more they hurry, the less time for questions.

Faces.

Curious. Tired. Annoyed.

"Watch out! Emergency coming through."

Faint giggles come from the wheelchair.

"Shh."

Everyone moves aside. The woman just looks too wretched, the way she is hanging in her chair.

Lalita parks Mrs. Malinowski behind some pieces of furniture waiting to be repaired. They are fixed to the wall with straps. "Don't move." Not that she can anyway.

She turns down the corridor that leads to the offices. This is a dangerous spot, since all sorts of officers mill around here. HR folks. Machinists. Safety. Security.

She slips into her office. Nike is on a video call with Miami in the adjacent conference room. She'll have to risk it. All in, now or never.

A moment later, she has managed to just barely wedge the wheelchair into the windowless office. She locks the door from the inside, drops into the office chair, and activates the four CCTV monitors.

"I can't see anything," Mrs. Malinowski moans.

Is her head sinking even farther down onto her chest, or is Lalita imagining things? The woman reminds her of a little bird, a bird preparing to die.

Nonsense.

She pulls the wheelchair next to her, as close as possible. With her left hand, she holds the mouse, and with her right, she carefully reaches her arm around the head, places her hand on the forehead, and gently pulls.

"Harder!" She is greedy. Greedy to look ahead, to finally see a piece of the world again.

Right, that is as far as she will stretch.

And go.

Lalita clicks her way through the cameras. She has no access to the material inside the casino, but the casino has two entrances. In a manner of speaking, it forms the heart of the ship, since there is no way around it. Everything is designed in order to drive the passengers through here, like flies; the weak ones get stuck and sucked dry.

She activates both cameras and then a third, which monitors the adjacent space: the lobby bar and elevators.

"There! My sister." Lalita can see the woman only from behind. She holds herself very straight. Indefinite age. She totters inside.

Eleven P.M.

Midnight.

Lalita fast-forwards.

At some point, much later, Jo appears on the screen.

Exits again almost immediately, fetches a drink from the bar and downs it while walking. Goes back in.

Out, in, out, in.

You're drinking too much, Jo. What are you up to?

Short pause. Mrs. Malinowski crumples again, like a marionette without a string. Her painful groans tug at Lalita's heartstrings. She stretches her knotted shoulders.

Move on. We're running out of time.

Okay. Forward. The sister appears again. A hard woman, rich and old. She makes the hair on Lalita's arms stand on end. A mighty opponent.

"Follow her. Stay on Wiltrud."

How can this crooked, delicate creature stand up against that one? It's just not possible. Lalita lets her fingers fly across the keys, as Wiltrud moves from camera to camera. Into the elevator. Down the corridor. To her suite. Door closes.

That was it. We got it wrong.

Maybe she found the guitar pick somewhere.

Empty corridor.

Back to the casino?

"No. Wait."

What's the point?

Forward.

"I'm sorry, Lalita." Yes, sure, she is sorry. This bent old woman feels sorry for her, because Jo is now staggering down the corridor instead of staying with her. Through the camera's fish-eye lens, he looks completely lost. He looks up briefly, and her hand twitches. Why didn't you say anything, Jo?

Move on.

Move on.

Let him pass the door.

Jo stops and knocks quietly. Wiltrud opens the door.

Jo disappears inside the suite.

Lalita has bitten her lip so hard that it bleeds. She can't wipe it off, because her hand is still holding up the woman's head. The other hand is on the mouse, as if grafted onto it.

Keep going.

The door opens, and Jo comes out, rushing down the corridor as if being chased by ghosts. The sister follows, her hair down. What's in her hand?

Zoom in.

Money. Hundred-euro notes.

Onward.

They argue in the corridor, and he takes the money. Again that glance upward, as if he knew you would be watching this later, Lalita. As if it were staged just for you. Why, Jo? Why are you doing this?

He takes the woman's hand, and she follows him.

Into the elevator. They head up silently.

Deck 12. There they are. Jo pulls her forward, up to the grassy golf area. The green glows brightly in the cold light of the ship's floodlights. Lalita sees its bright toxic green, even though the CCTV footage is black and white.

The surveillance camera is mounted right in the middle of the foredeck. The scene unfolds before this central perspective, like a tableau, as if it were onstage.

Jo laughs. He seems happy, too happy.

They dance.

From right to left, out of the picture.

Next camera. Portside. Lalita is hyped up. She can't feel her arm anymore, the one holding the old woman's head up.

The couple in black and white is dancing, seen diagonally from above. A silent movie. Bizarre. They are dancing right above the side windows of the bridge.

Lalita zooms in.

Wiltrud's eyes are closed, but Jo's are not.

He lets her go. She stumbles.

He looks into the camera. That look again.

He pulls her toward him from behind.

He kisses her.

Then Jo lets himself tip backward over the railing.

Or did she push him?

The surveillance is completely useless.

You see everything, but you know nothing.

Cry, Lalita.

What else can you do?

RAFT (NO NAME)

Karim Yacine

Pick up.

Pick up.

Pick up.

The signal is growing weaker.

We've got to get out of here as fast as possible.

Karim is crouching under the tarp, clutching the engine's tiller handle. He has three pieces of thin plastic sheeting with him: One for the five in the bow. One for the teacher, Abdelmjid, the sleeping cousin, and the injured man. One for himself and the engine. The two boys have caps and act like hardened men.

Flying blind.

He can't see anything, with or without the tarp. The boat underneath him wobbles up and down, as if it were made of liquid. The motor greedily devours the fresh gas and rattles at full torque. The only thing Karim can hear is the roaring of the storm, but his hand can feel the vibration, and he registers the machine's power in his body. He stares at his cell phone. The GPS is still activated. You have to stay on course. The Spanish mainland lies to the west. That's where we want to go.

What's up with Zohra? Why won't she pick up?

Karim would give anything to turn back the past hour and toss his fear overboard, which has gripped him during this crossing. It is the first time he has ever been frightened, and the fear makes him feel small and cowardly.

He's afraid that Zohra will leave him.

He's afraid of the detention center at Murcia.

He's afraid of death.

He's afraid of the moment he'll finally be alone with Zohra, alone in the house in the mountains, of the moment when Zohra will lift the blanket that covers the Black Decade. Her questions, which will stretch on forever, because there are no answers.

France is a neutral zone, a transit region. We can become other people there, even though we've become who we are today because of the French. A serpentine eight with no end.

Breaking the silence.

"Breaking the silence" is a good expression.

Something breaks forever.

Don't set her free.

Fight for your life.

That young Frenchman with the canister full of gas has given him life. Take it, make something out of it. Take it as a sign. You and Zohra's future lies in France, not in Algeria. Algeria will kill your love, which will suffocate under its large, dark blanket.

It thunders.

Sagging with rain, the tarp presses around his body. Karim feels as if he is shrink-wrapped in cellophane. I don't want to suffocate.

With his left hand, he yanks off the tarp, and the wind and rain pelt his skin.

Alive!

With this realization, his mind switches back to full power. Don't just think about yourself. You have ten men and a severely injured person in this boat. Bring them to safety. Give them freedom.

For the first time, he looks behind him. The cruise ship, already far away, disappears into a wall of rain. A flash of lightning flickers across the dark gray sky. All it takes is a fraction of a second, as the raft rides a wave crest. An orange glow. The sea rescue boat is here. It is fast and has the stronger engines.

But Karim has the advantage. We're the invisible ones, *les invisibles*. With all of your technology, your radar, your speedboats, you can't detect us. We can hide between the waves.

As the *zodiac* plunges once more into a wave trough, Karim heaves to. Now he can stay parallel to the wave, as long as he maintains his speed. The GPS vanishes into his pocket, and his inner radar kicks back on.

He scans the sky. Give me a bright spot, just a shade of difference. The teacher pokes his head out from under the tarp, as if he senses that something has changed.

"I'm taking you ashore!" Karim yells.

He no longer feels the motor.

He's surfing.

He's flying.

Westward.

That is where we'll reach land, on a black beach that can't be missed from the sea. A black beach that he had discovered on Google Maps, one that has only a few houses, no harbor.

This beach is the gateway to everything we need, a future for all of you in the bow. A shop that peddles something other than just dates for Abdelmjid. Selective amnesia, perhaps at some point, for the cousin who lost his brother. The newest games for the kids from the quarter. French books for the teacher. A hospital for you, unknown friend.

And for you, Karim?

Will you be brave enough to ask Zohra for forgiveness?

Karim surfs.

Don't turn around.

After an eternity—minutes or hours?—a distant hill rises up out of the mist. It has to be an island. It appears to be floating in the air, over the sea.

Where are we?

Then he sees a beacon to the left of the island, its flame licking up high into the sky. See, it looks like it's ripping the sky apart. Mountains materialize out of nothing.

He chokes the engine.

He will very slowly steer the *zodiac* between this island's boulders. This is where he will wait until darkness comes.

THE FOLLOWING NIGHT

Sybille Malinowski

Sybille sees the man's shoes and suspects what is about to come. He stands spread-legged, so she cannot get by with the wheelchair.

"Good evening, my ladies!" She can sense the grin suspended on his face. She has always valued good social manners; they are simply in your blood. But nothing revolts her more than phony cordiality. Mechanical artificialities are no different from the dancing bears at the circus. She hears Wiltrud respond curtly. This is where they have something in common. If he now just wouldn't—

"Wash your hands, please." He stands straight like the number 1 and will not let them pass until they hold their hands under the disinfectant dispensers. The wheelchair stops right in front of the plastic column, and Wiltrud's hands unwillingly accept their fate.

Sybille giggles quietly. All that sinfully expensive hand cream is going straight to the devil.

Thanks to plastic surgery and expensive cosmetics, on her good days and in flattering light, her little sister looks like she is in her midfifties. However, her hands are those of an old woman.

"Do it, Sybille!"

All right! I finished up a while ago. It is just that my hands have not really gotten started. See how they tremble uncontrollably, like little animals, completely independent from me and my wishes.

Oh, the sanitizer is cold.

My hands flutter, and half of the liquid trickles onto the rug. Rightly so.

She is pushed on. Good thing that their table is up high, right at the balustrade, so she can gaze down on the heads of the diners on the first and second levels.

And on Claus.

Good evening, Claus, my friend.

Here is an admirer who suits her taste, consummate old school. The photograph hangs at the center of the flight of stairs leading down: the shipowner Claus Goldstein in a tuxedo, leaning nonchalantly on the railing of a passenger steamer, his passenger steamer. The America-Europe line, between Hamburg and New York.

Oh, how she had loved traveling on it! Wiltrud and her husband had been among the first passengers. This was during the time she was working in the medical store, to help finance Ulrich's med school. No need to mention the two children.

Claus Goldstein was a figure practically plucked from a fairy tale. Wealthy Jewish family. Fed the half-starved residents of Hamburg out of his private soup kitchen after World War I. Became unbelievably rich from auto imports from the US. The first passenger ships between Europe and Palestine, one of which carried Max and his sister away from the Nazis to safety. What twists and turns human fate can hold. Sybille never would have guessed. This was the Goldstein who had conveyed her cousin into a future on the other side of Auschwitz, the Goldstein whom the Nazis arrested and dispossessed. Two years later, he immigrated to the US. His wife practically bought his freedom at the last second. It was this Goldstein who, after the war, had no greater dream than to revitalize the passenger ship traffic between America and Europe. This Goldstein was the founder of the company that is now a corporation with the name of Gold Cruises, headquartered in Miami.

"Sybille!" Wiltrud hisses from where she is sitting across from her.

The table next to theirs has been occupied since Southampton by a British couple, along with their son, daughter-in-law, and two grandchildren. The grandparents look like they have leaped out of one of those awful American TV series, so sleek.

"Good evening," the couple purrs. The others are missing. Without being asked, they report that the rest of them are down on the ice rink. This is addressed directly to Wiltrud, of course. Wheelchair-bound Sybille is shunned like a leper.

The conversation burbles on: Gold Cruise Card, Star Lounge, free drinks. Eventual delay in Mallorca, because of that incident this afternoon.

"Incident?" Sybille throws herself into the conversation as abruptly as she can. "But they're people! People who need help, not—"

The woman brusquely interrupts. "It's just irritating when you're the last ship to arrive. Someone's always snatching the best things right out from under your nose. Isn't that right, darling?"

The waiter walks up, a new one this evening. The old one was Alexander from Greece.

A black man. His name is Oke. Something's wrong with his posture; maybe he has a foot malposition, but that could be treated. Oke also speaks to Wiltrud, reeling off the usual recommendations from the head chef. She puts her glasses on decisively, studying the menu, the wines.

Oke waits.

Sybille studies his feet. Shoe inlays would certainly be helpful.

"What would you like to start with this evening, ladies?"

Wiltrud orders. For starters, two seafood ceviches; for the main course, grilled fillet of plaice with potato-artichoke au gratin for my sister and saddle of lamb with the thyme reduction for me. And the sauvignon blanc for both of us. Wiltrud always orders the second most inexpensive wine on the menu. Wine costs extra.

"I don't want anything."

"What?" She imagines Oke's gaze flying between her and her sister.

"Sybille!" Wiltrud hisses again.

"I don't want to eat anything."

"But, madam, the food is—"

"The food is free, I know. I just don't want to eat anything." Sybille has prepared herself for this moment: brace yourself on both hands.

Head, get up.

Okay, a couple of centimeters.

She sees the Royals' martini glasses floating through the air. Sybille calls them the Royals because they've bored them with their incessant chatter about how important the monarchy is for England since the very first evening.

Sybille has had enough.

The battle with utensils gets harder each day, not to mention the stares that she does not see but can feel, like pinpricks.

How unpleasant.

And the waiter, whether Alexander or Oke, who whisks away her totally soiled napkin with an elegant flick of the wrist.

It is enough. Starting tomorrow, she will dine in her suite.

"I'm not eating."

Wiltrud, there you are. I'm not sure how long I can hold my head up.

"Be quiet!" she interrupts her sister, who is about to start lecturing her. Oke slips away. "Listen to me. Get that thing out, your tablet."

Wiltrud obeys, astonishingly. She picks up her Gucci bag and pulls it out.

"Email." Oh, if only her voice were as steady as it used to be. This is only half as much fun as it could have been. "And you, mind your own business!"

The Royals jerk back. I think this is the first time they have noticed me. Yes, I'm a thinking person!

Wiltrud's finger glides nervously across the screen.

Sybille's neck hurts unbearably.

She mentally lets it all go.

Her hand reaches for the balustrade. Ah, now I've got Goldstein back in view. Is he smiling a little? Does my little show amuse you, Claus? He winks at her.

He winked. Really.

Wiltrud has surely found the email with the film by now. The entire humiliating scene.

Her young lover.

The end of a dream.

My God, Wiltrud.

Sybille studies Claus Goldstein and imagines the two of them dancing a sublime waltz under the chandelier. Magnificent.

"What's this, Sybille?" Wiltrud whispers.

"We're playing a little game." Focus on your voice, Sybille. Speak loudly and clearly.

She has thought it all through.

The cruise ends at Monte Carlo, and Wiltrud won't want to skip the famous casino there.

"We're playing one final game, little sister. All or nothing."

Your house. Your fortune. Your freedom. Everything on a single card. In Palma, we will go to a notary, and you will sign everything over to me. In Barcelona, I will have a bill made out to me from my bank, and in Monte Carlo, we will gamble. If by the end of the night you have won, I will agree to go to a care facility, as you have proposed. If you lose, you will move in with me, into my beloved house on the Alster. No worries, you won't have to wipe my backside. Others can do that better than you, but you will keep being my companion. Go with me to the opera. Occasionally go on trips, as long as that is still possible for me. All according to my conditions.

You think it's ridiculous, Wiltrud? Really?

Well, the Hamburg tabloid papers will certainly find this video ridiculous as well, especially once I provide them with a few more details.

How you tried desperately to buy the love of this young man.

A woman of your background, Wiltrud.

You should be ashamed.

Seamus Clarke

Is the ship swaying, or is it me?

Seamus can't fit his bloody Sea Pass into the slit in the cabin door.

The door to the cabin across the way flies open. "Miles?" a dark-haired woman cries, her breasts nearly tumbling out of her robe. American, Seamus assumes. Face already over-hauled once. He follows her gaze down the empty passage.

"It's just me here, luv," he grunts.

Only now does she seem to register his presence. She mumbles something, and *bang*, she's gone.

It's always that way. Pure class warfare is raging on this ship. Those who can afford a suite can dine whenever they want, along with unlimited access to loungers on the sun deck and free cocktails. No doubt there's a crew member, name of Pawel or Stanley, on constant call to kiss their asses as needed, too. Anyone who pays for an outer cabin with a balcony gets tickets to dinner at eight and a wide grin from the cabin steward, along with carte blanche to send dirty looks at the people across the way.

Kelly and his brothers meant well.

Dinner at six. A cabin with a window.

Some people don't even have that.

Eventually the bloody door opens and he gets into the cabin. Is it day or night right now? He's already forgotten. The window lets out on the shopping promenade.

There's no daylight inside here.

The designer watch sale is still going on in front of the jewelry shop, as men rip blingy watches off each other's wrists. Whose is bigger? Go ahead, show me yours. Credit cards flash.

Kelly is sitting in front of the café with a couple of girls from Dublin, and she isn't missing out on the show, as they sip colorful drinks with slices of fruit on the rims. Her gaze darts up to him, and she waves.

Seamus waves back. "Enjoy yourself, my girl." You've earned it.

He takes a step back and rams into the edge of the bed, as something brushes against his shoulder.

"Damn it!"

Today it's a monkey.

A different animal every evening, twisted and turned out of towels. They'll do anything for a good tip. The monkey rocks quietly to and fro.

It is far from cute.

He avoids the animal's stare and sits down at the desk, before connecting the camera to his laptop and copying the pictures over. Familiar movements. Seamus is a techie, according to Kelly. In the mornings, when she is at work and he can't sleep anymore, he fiddles around on the computer for hours, loading things on his Facebook page and exchanging stuff with friends. Follows his favorite channels. Checks out what's going on in the Republic. Listens to music.

He wouldn't have been able to set one foot on this ship without the flat rate. Poor Kelly, everything costs extra. It'll be a pretty penny when it's all said and done.

When the dark Frenchwoman at the reception desk explained to them that an extra tip of twelve dollars was expected, Kelly had grown very pale around the nose. Per person per day! And always with that smile on her lips. She looked like a supermodel, dragging you to Hades with a smile.

Seamus had wrapped his arms around his Kelly. "Forget about it, girl. I'll take care of the rest." A couple of extra shifts should cover it.

Copy process complete.

Now he can start the upload. For the trip, he'd set up a special YouTube channel. "You owe us that, little brother. Every evening, we want to see something from the world of the rich and beautiful." He can visualize them all sitting around up there at Rob's, since he has the biggest house, right at the foot of Black Mountain. It is all thanks to Rob's successful trucking company.

"Oh, boys, today you'll get something special."

That was the belly flop contest. And then... He scrolls through the pictures.

Ah, there it is.

Man, that's quite the jiggle you've got, Seamus Clarke! Coming down with Parkinson's or something? Anyone who watches that will get dizzy.

He pauses the video clip to figure out the exact number of boys in the boat to add later to the comment box.

It's eleven.

Zoom out.

The mob at the railing, and then the men out there on the sea again. Two worlds. Unequal worlds.

Seamus wishes that he'd brought a beer up with him.

Next clip.

There's the boat that went out to them. Applause. He'd filmed that from Deck 4. Now they're coming back, mission accomplished.

Next clip.

Ah yes, there he is back out on deck. That had to have been right before the storm, though he can't really remember. He'd already thrown a few back by then.

Seamus grins.

Wait a sec.

Stop.

He counts.

Again.

Twelve.

Go back to the other clip.

Eleven.

Wide-awake now. Like in the hospital, he can see everything. Earlier, it had been eleven. Then the lifeboat goes out, and then it is twelve.

Seamus leans back.

One more on the raft.

What does that mean?

There is only one explanation.

Just one.

Someone from this ship is now out on the raft.

"Kevin."

Utter rot. Pull yourself together, Seamus Clarke. Kevin is dead and has been for the past thirty-seven years.

He turns around and stares at the dumb monkey.

You're just made out of towels.

There are no such things as ghosts.

Seamus thinks.

Why didn't I bring a beer, damn it?

What to do?

You have to do something.

Are there smugglers on board, or something like that? Not on a pleasure boat. Or maybe?

Is it possible to find someone on this bloody internet who could answer a simple question for him? Seamus clicks through his 243 friends, but they are all old codgers.

No, wait. Stop.

There, Fiona, Rob's second oldest. She is studying law in Bologna. He scrolls through her profile. Hadn't she recently posted a link to an NGO that focuses on refugees in the Mediterranean? Yep, Fiona's a real little troublemaker, just like her father. Always taking on the high and mighty.

His fingers fly across the keys. "Take a look at this, Fiona." He posts the YouTube link and writes her a short note.

Send.

This will be something for her to chew on for a while, young and full of revolutionary energy. You can't help feeling sorry for the young ones. They don't know where to go with it. That wasn't a problem we had.

Seamus stands up, stretches, and goes to the window.

The last of the designer watches have swapped owners.

Kelly's drink is almost empty.

Let's go, old friend. The lady wants to kick up her heels yet today. Let's enjoy life, Kelly, love of my life.

The Irish way.

And next year, can we maybe go back to Donegal?

Do you remember how they used to always search us on the stretch between Derry and the Republic?

Every single time.

Roadblocks. They would see our names in the passports, and then it was two hours of shenanigans, at least. Once we were back on the road, we could breathe deeply. Out of Belfast, out of the insanity. The purest paradise.

Donegal.

Swimming in the ice-cold sea until we froze our bums off.

Tinkering around in our old camper.

Visiting Rob and the others in their campers down the road.

Going to the pub in the evenings, and stumbling into ditches on the way back, because we were that drunk.

"True, old friend?" He gives the towel monkey a shove. It swings.

And swings.

And swings.

Long after Seamus has left.

Nikhil Mehta

Nike works through his program very diligently, refusing to indulge in even one moment of dreaming or high spirits. Is he supposed to waste his time dancing around here or what?

Before every assignment, he spends hours putting together a plan with his personal trainer in Mumbai, which he then executes, no matter what.

At some point, the party is over.

Then it's his time. Off goes the uniform.

Ninety minutes alone with your body.

Ten minutes of interval rowing to warm up.

He adjusts the leg press so the pain in his thighs sets in immediately. Fifteen repetitions followed by short breaks.

The spa area is mostly empty at this time; the guests, even the athletic ones, are off stuffing themselves. There's one sun-tanned Northern European, somewhere between sixty and eighty, lying motionless in the whirlpool. Occasionally, he takes a sip from his cocktail. Alcohol in the fitness area. Gold Cruises knows no limits where money is concerned.

Move on.

Over to the negative bench press. Nike carefully spreads his towel on top of it and hooks himself in. Now he has an upside-down view of the circular room.

Sit-ups. Fifteen. Short pause. Another set. Pause.

A girl is working out on the cross stepper in the back of the room. Guilty conscience, too fat. She had dinner at six and will go get some pizza later.

Move on.

Back and biceps on the vertical traction. Three sets of fifteen.

Dumbbell rowing, twenty-five kilos.

He feels the burn in his biceps. Good.

Is the guy in the whirlpool still alive? The model of the SS *Spirit of Gold* hangs above him.

Another coincidence. Is there such a thing as a coincidence? In the never-ending cycle of life, death, and reincarnation? The *Spirit of Gold* is the mother of all ships in the Gold Cruises fleet.

Nike saw her die.

It was 1996, and they were on the beach of Alang, Gujarat. Nike, his brother, and his father were there for Sangh Shiksha Varga. An endless, wonderful summer. Alang is the biggest ship graveyard in the world. *The world dumps its garbage here with us,* his father liked to say. *One day we will play right at the top. Believe me, son.*

He sits down on the bench. Curl bar, three sets of fifteen curls. Two guys come in. Envious glances. Yes, take a look. The six-pack is real. The funny thing is that nobody recognizes him. You're always just one of those dark guys in uniform. No need to remember the actual face, but here in the gym, we're equals.

You always meet twice.

He bounces back to his feet, over to the bars. Three sets of fifteen.

Nike is ready for the highlight. Slowly over to the bench, then sets the weights.

Thirty.

Fifty.

He knows they are watching, the two guys.

Sixty.

Tough, that's really tough.

Made it. Once more.

Good thing he had taken that booster. If you take it half an hour before you start your workout, you are not only awake and energized. You are focused.

Eight.

Nine.

Come on, one more time.

Ten.

The sweat is streaming into his eyes.

He grabs the sixteen-kilo dumbbells and does his set of flies.

Last thing, the treadmill. He walks slowly around the semicircle of silent machines and carefully selects one after checking the view.

Yes, that works.

Intervals. He starts at level twelve, and the machine does the rest for him. It will advance him up to sixteen at regular intervals. Up. Down.

In front of him, the starry sky, a panorama view. The storm has totally vanished.

Nike runs himself into a trance.

The moon is almost full.

In front of me, a silver belt extends right out to the horizon.

A path.

My way to the stars.

The email has finally arrived. Acquittal.

Free.

Free of guilt.

After twelve years. He had been a young policeman in Gujarat, India.

We were told to look the other way.

That came from way up, they said.

If they call and ask for help, hang up.

Twenty-four hours.

He had looked away.

He runs.

He runs along.

Faster now. The belt beneath him is racing. Sixteen.

The belt stretches before him, as if made of spun silver. Infinite.

A follower.

The mob raged out of control.

We'll kill them. We'll chop them into pieces. We'll set their houses on fire. We'll take revenge.

Nobody put themselves in its path.

We will take what we're owed. We are Hindus. We are India. Jai Ram.

The boy, who'd been persuaded by the NGOs to accuse him, can't walk anymore, but there is nothing physically wrong with him. He feels guilty, they say, because he was the only one from his family to survive. A fake, if you ask me. They say he lives with relatives now, safe and sound, and will be a man soon. Maybe he'll have the courage to come look him in the eye

Nikhil Mehta. Acquitted.

For lack of evidence.

Fifteen televisions switch on at the same time. Franz, who is on night duty in the spa, appears in his line of vision. "Sorry, officer. They want the news."

Nike smiles. It's all right.

The spell is broken. Human voices fill the spa. Putin appears on the screen above his treadmill, smiling too.

Nike keeps smiling.

His phone rings.

The treadmill stops.

Léon Moret

Léon kisses Mado, who sparkles brighter than the artificial star-spangled sky in the Star Lounge. Her beauty takes his breath away. She's a queen.

Mado's gig will start any minute. She likes transformations: uniform and glasses in the morning, femme fatale at night. This sideline is her real passion. Mado sings Nina Simone covers for the discerning audience.

She takes a step back from him and slowly walks in between the tables. The old geezers stare at her, as the women turn away, humbled by her beauty.

Oh man, this woman is pure sex. Léon wants to scramble after her, tear off her sequined gown, and fuck her, right here, in front of all these people. Look here, this is my wife.

His wife. Forever.

They got married in Las Vegas. Flew in just a couple of friends and Mado's sister. Her parents didn't want to come: *We are simple people, that is not our world.* And Georges and Sylvie? In Las Vegas? Never.

That was okay. It was our world, our party, our life. When the sun rose, she sang for him and him alone. A naked African goddess. Léon swore that he would always worship her. In the autumn, when the caravan of Gold Cruises ships moves back over to the Caribbean, they will go ashore at Martinique.

Mado's family is from there, and they will have a huge party with her clan.

"You'll be the only white person there, Léon, my darling."

So what?

I belong to you, Mado. Play with me, do whatever you like.

She stands on the small stage up there. The spotlight comes on, and the pianist begins to play. Mado blows him a kiss, as the randy geezers crane their necks.

Feel free to take a look.

Do you see the stripes on my uniform?

He turns and goes to the door. For the next few hours, she belongs to the others. Her voice follows him until the door closes. He pauses for a moment. He is suspended between the pool deck and the video screen above. Music videos are playing on mute, and the DJ is in the middle of a set on the small stage below. A couple of girls are dancing, as a boy jumps into the pool fully dressed. People will keep lining up at the cocktail bar as long as it's still happy hour. The Tunisian barkeeper looks up and smiles at him. What was her name again?

Léon yearns for the dark silence of the bridge. He looks at his watch. It's not worth playing another round of *FIFA*. The PlayStation can stay off for today. He goes over to the elevator and waits for the glass cabin. A couple gets out, about the same age as Georges and Sylvie.

What a thought.

During his first season on the Mediterranean, he had called them from somewhere. "Would you like to take a trip?" Léon was sure that Fabian would enjoy being on board, since he loved colorful, bright things. "Hey, you can

MERLE KRÖGER

tour Europe without having to find a hotel that'll accommodate the wheelchair."

Sylvie laughed. "Léon, are you serious? Georges on a cruise. He'd sooner go on a crusade."

Georges grabbed the receiver from her hand—"Do you know how many tons of diesel your polluting monster chugs every week, asshole?"—and hung up.

Léon enters the code, and the door to the bridge opens. The Gurkha smiles. Léon smiles back. He sees Mehta's and the captain's silhouettes against the illuminated curtain. He walks past. It sounds like trouble: "....an overboard, Mehta! The Spanish doctor reported it straight to Miami. Do you know—"

Léon steps toward the window. Does that mean the Syrian is already in the hospital?

He listens to his inner voice, more curious than worried.

Onboard security is definitely Mehta's baby.

Wow.

If he got busted, that would be mind-blowing. And totally deserved.

Léon strolls around to the starboard side. The less he picks up of the conversation, the better for him. The sky is full of stars, and it is only three more days until the full moon. The white shimmer on the dark water reminds him of Mado's sequined dress.

Mado.

Beacons at ten to twelve. The Spanish coast. If his inner GPS is not mistaken, that is around the location of La Mancha. Somewhere out there in the darkness lies the beach that poisoned Fabian in his mother's womb.

Portmán.

The great thing is that Georges got his revenge in the end. The village suffocated in its own poisonous sludge, which gradually blocked up the harbor and filled the whole bay.

And now they can't get rid of it. EU project status aborted. Private investors aborted.

Eternally contaminated.

Uh-oh, the captain's temper is really turning foul now.

Léon smiles.

Mehta's done for, suffocating in his own poisonous brew as well.

"Change of guard!"

Instinctively, he snaps to attention.

Here we go.

One more time.

Luke Skywalker is back on watch.

CARTAGENA HARBOR | SPAIN

Diego Martínez

Asclepius, the Greek god of death and healing. His temple once stood up there on the highest of the five hills. He was adopted by the Romans and brought to Carthago Nova, the capital of their Iberian empire. Nobody knows why they built a temple to him here of all places. Perhaps it had been a stormy crossing, or there had been illness on board.

Asclepius is a bearded fellow with a stick, around which an Aesculapian snake twines. This is not the only reason Diego feels close to the god. The logo for the Spanish sea rescue service features a crown hovering over an anchor and a twisted rope, which reminds him of Asclepius. Also in Diego's life, death and rescue are only millimeters apart from each other. Today, death wins.

Diego hoses down the *Salvamar Rosa* as she floats in the full shine of her powerful spotlights in the basin of the Cartagena Port Authority. The Guardia Civil speedboats are hiding in the darkness. *Rosa*'s orange paint gleams as he caresses her with the stream of water. Section by section, he makes her sparkle. She is demanding, his *Rosa*. She makes her temperament felt whenever the *patrón* pushes both turbines to full throttle. She doesn't have a propeller like the other ships, for safety reasons. She has rocket engines instead.

Patiently, he pivots the stream back to the left; only a small strip still needs to be done. He is not obsessed with his boat—his last girlfriend had been wrong about that. She was from the city, and there was no way that could have ended well.

Only the wife of a fisherman could understand what binds the men of Escombreras to their boats. Whenever his father cleans the *Florentina* or his uncle the *Maria*, that is the time when a man comes to terms with himself and leaves his fears with his boat. She is his confidante and knows everything about him.

Diego drops the hose and picks up a rag to rub out any remaining oil spots. Cartagena Bay lies silently underneath the almost full moon. Where are the men they spent the day looking for? Where are the other people he has searched for in vain? There have to be hundreds of them by this point.

The travelers on the *pateras* pass along to each other the number for the sea rescue service in Cartagena. "If you're in trouble, call them." Floating in the middle of the sea, they stumble across some cell network or another and then call up to the switchboard.

Do you understand? They can call, but they might still be lost if we can't find them fast enough. They could still die of dehydration. They could still drown. They could still be plowed down by a freighter. They have to cross two shipping channels between Algeria and the Spanish coast, at night, without lights. Invisible to every radar.

He angrily rubs at the last stubborn spot. All of these lost people are silhouettes, like the graffiti on the harbor wall, like the ones in their overalls who are bussed to Murcia.

They have to stay here.

I can't take you with me.

Diego straightens up. He hangs the rag over the shiny metal railing to dry and goes inside to switch off the lamps.

The *Rosa* will take care of them. She is a kindhearted soul, and her diva attitude is just for show. She had gathered Zohra in and offered her comfort and sleep.

Zohra. A face like a Madonna. A Madonna of pain and sadness, with eyes older than the rest of her body. She climbed down from the deck as if in slow motion, as if she had to force every movement.

The *patrón* had taken care of all the paperwork with her. She looked around and raised her hand, before slowly working her way down the pier and vanishing.

And he? He had stood there like an idiot, holding the hose. He stares into the darkness for a moment, wishing he could rewind the film and she would suddenly reappear.

Diego steps back on land.

The *patrón* yawns as he sits at the computer in the workshop. "Algeria," he comments as Diego enters. He looks meaningfully over the rim of his reading glasses, which he has been wearing on a chain around his neck for the past few months.

"Sure, where else would they come from?" Diego is weary and in no mood to chat. The *patrón* likes to talk shit—that's his way.

He jerks his head toward the door. "No. Her."

Diego coils the hose neatly and hangs it on its hook. The helmet goes on top of the shelf, the gloves right next to it.

Her.

The information fights its way to the surface of his consciousness.

Her. Zohra.

He turns around. The *patrón* is grinning smugly, leaning back and patting his stomach, across which the buttons of his so-called captain's uniform are straining.

"I gave her twenty euros out of the coffee till so she can reach the consulate general in Alicante. Papers, money—everything's gone."

Out of the coffee till. He would never give her his own money. Diego nods and is seized by a sense of unease. Zohra. All alone out there. He sees her again in his mind, how she disappeared into the darkness.

He is already half out of his overalls. The locker. Pants, T-shirt, hooded jacket. Quick, stuff it all in. Grab car keys.

"Why the hurry?" The *patrón* flourishes a bottle of good brandy, Carlos I. It has become something of a ritual after a job well done.

"My father," Diego murmurs. "Soccer game on TV. Promised."

He strides around the corner, breaking into a run as soon as he is out of sight. Down the pier—it strikes him as endlessly long today. His car is parked under the tin roof next to the unloading area for the rafts they haul in. Door opens. Key goes in the ignition.

I have to find her.

He reverses and tears off in a squeal of tires.

"Where are you off to in such a hurry?" blares one of the loudspeakers close to the gate. "Gotta go or something?" The laughter of the man on shift up at the switchboard mixes with the rattling of the gate as it slowly opens.

Much too slowly.

He drives through, brakes.

She could be anywhere.

Long gone.

Walked into the city.

Think, Diego. What would you do?

Away from here. Too dark.

Somewhere where there is light. Among people.

He drives slowly past the empty parking lots along the fishing harbor. Up ahead, the end of the promenade. That is where the people and restaurants are. A summer evening. Yacht owners drinking wine and eating paella.

Wait a sec, what's that?

An Espace that had not been here before. There, just a shadow, fumbling with the driver's door.

Diego reverses until his headlights illuminate the scene. The figure turns around, blinded. Framed by her headscarf, she has the eyes of the Madonna.

His heart pounds faster.

He steps out.

She glares at him furiously. He doesn't understand a word.

Walks toward her.

Grasps her shoulders. Very cautiously. "Come home." His voice sounds husky.

She is now perfectly still.

His parents will be shocked by this late guest.

She takes a step toward him.

Suddenly, Diego has to laugh. "The Spanish Republicans—" he begins, but is unsure how to continue. Whatever. His hand reaches for hers.

The Republican fleet escaped twice to Algeria.

It is now time to return the favor.

CASTELLÓN DE LA PLANA HARBOR | SPAIN

Oleksij Lewtschenko

He's standing on the pier.

Olek feels like a midget, like a newly hatched chick. It is the first time in weeks he has felt solid ground under his feet. The ground sways. Sailors know this phenomenon—the ship won't let them go.

The word SIOBHAN stands in white letters across the ship's black stern. He is standing right in front of her, at her ass, so to speak. The tailwind blows directly across the containers; Dmitri had landed the *Siobhan* at the pier with remarkable flair. A German freighter bobs in front of her, and right behind her, the sea jetty ends.

The cranes are running up and down above the German vessel. A Jeep from the Guardia Civil blasts past Olek's nose and comes to a screeching stop at the end of the pier.

Olek is familiar with this nocturnal drama among men. First the truck with the workers who will moor the boat pulls up, then lots of yelling. *Throw me the rope now. Pull, you jackasses. What kind of assholes are you, haven't you ever berthed a boat before?* Then the pilot disembarks, as the Guardia Civil arrives and checks the papers on everyone who leaves the ship and enters European soil.

One guy steps down and covers the distance between them with wide strides. They know each other. A short flip through his naval passport. That was it. "Enjoy your vacation, buddy."

Olek growls his thanks.

Vacation.

Dmitri. You can't do this. After so many years.

There is a lot to take care of on the bridge after the docking, long after the engines have been cut off. His engines. He has repaired each of the nine blocks more than once, with his flashlight between his teeth and his wrench in hand. His *Siobhan* runs smoothly, and the engine room gleams in pale silver.

Come on, Dmitri, old friend. We've been through so much together. It can't end this way. A couple of words in farewell. A hug between men.

No politics on board this ship. That was your motto. Let that still hold true for tonight, too.

The last six months, day after day, the silence in the officers' mess. Three Russians and two Ukrainians. News, day after day. Good for you, bad for us. I sometimes came close to losing it with you.

But we got through it. Remember when that storm blew up in the Gulf of Marseille? I thought our trusty *Siobhan* was going to crack down the middle as our entire load of containers crashed down in the wave trough. It was ten, twelve meters, no shit.

Remember when the stabilizers failed, and we were suddenly listing at 9 percent toward starboard and had to balance the tanks by hand? Remember when we found the Algerians in the container last winter? And how the Spaniards didn't want to let them on land, but sent over two cops instead to accompany them back to where they'd come from? That is why we celebrated Christmas with two Spanish policemen in Oran. Our legendary suckling pig à la Manila? Remember that? It was a great party.

Dmitri, you can't do this. Not this way.

Olek looks up to the illuminated bridge. A tiny island of light. How many hours had they spent up there together, staring out?

At the sea.

At the containers.

No politics on this ship.

And he, Olek, was the one who broke that law, when he returned to the bridge.

The storm had fit the mood.

Thunder.

"Hi, Chief. There you are." Dmitri with his binoculars in hand. "It's quite the weather we've got out there."

Dmitri read the letter out loud. Lightning.

"You aren't seriously going to do that."

But I am, Dmitri.

I want to, I have to.

Are you already on the radio with the crewing agency in Cyprus to tell them you need a new chief engineer by tomorrow? And no Ukrainians, please. It won't be easy for poor Sergei. But since he lives in Ireland and knows our Odessa only from his parents' stories, it's not hard for him to shut out the politics.

We, however... Don't you understand, Dmitri? Your Putin turned us into nationalists. Until a year ago, my son had the Russian flag hanging up in his room. He liked everything that came from Russia. Europe could go hang itself, as far as we were concerned.

When I was home the last time, in late May, the flag was gone. I found a few charred bits of it in the garden. My son and I, we didn't need to talk about it. Instead, we went to the place where Odessa died, on May 2, 2014.

The union building went up in flames, and everyone told a different story. What happened there, Dmitri? You don't know? But your Putin does. He's a control freak who leaves nothing to chance. You think it could have been our people? Why not the American intelligence guys? The two of us, we'll never know. We weren't there. We're never there. We ride around on the sea, while everything goes to hell at home.

You want to know why so much went wrong over the past few weeks, Dmitri? The container that crashed through the opening. The empty tank right before we reached Barcelona. I can tell you. It doesn't matter anymore.

Earlier we'd raise a glass together, Dmitri, in the evenings on the bridge or after our meal in the officers' mess. I drink alone these days, secretly, between the containers. I'm drinking it up, Dmitri. The news from home, the Facebook videos that Irina sends me. Yesterday they unrolled a yellow-and-blue flag on the steps of Odessa, the Potemkin Steps.

I have to know where my place is, Dmitri. Then, perhaps, someday I can return. I'm going to war so my son and the other boys don't have to.

Here comes the taxi that the charter company sent. Take care, my friend. It's a shame your motto didn't apply this time: No politics on this ship.

One of the Filipinos raises the gangway with the crane. Olek now knows that Dmitri will not come. Who is the man in the overalls, wearing a helmet? He can't recognize him, and that irritates him. He needs to know the identity of the last person he will ever see on his ship, the one lifting his hand in farewell.

Olek raises his in return.

The taxi is waiting, motor running. He steps in. They drive beneath the cranes, the freighters to their left, the containers towering high, one on top of the other, to their right. Hanjin. Maersk. Hamburg-Süd. CMA CGM. Container dominoes. They played it often, at night on the bridge.

They've passed them and are driving along the narrow street between the terminal buildings and the house-high sheet piling.

I'm on the road to nowhere.

Is he imagining things, or is the street growing narrower? He tugs on his jacket collar. It's stuffy in here.

He opens the window.

Stop, turn around. Something is pulling him inexorably back to his ship.

I don't want to die.

The taxi races through the night.

Pause at the customs barrier. Papers again. Then the hand waving the taxi through.

Olek exhales.

We're out.

A traffic circle. Deserted.

"Want to go straight to your hotel?"

He puts it off. "No. Keep driving a little. Is there a good bar around here?"

The driver laughs. "Down that way, toward the beach." They drive along the harbor promenade and encounter a few late-night tourists.

"Please, stop here!"

The taxi brakes, and Olek gets out. "I'll take the suitcase myself, no worries." The car takes off with a rev of its engine.

Olek walks slowly toward the open door. Just as he is about to enter, two old women come out, one pushing a walker. No smiles are offered.

He steps into the church, suitcase in hand.

A painting above the altar of a boat bobbing under stormy clouds, helpless in the sea. The boat is carrying sailors in long white robes, just like the Arabs wear. Two of the sailors are clinging up high on the mast, and one of them is trying to reef the sail. Five others are pressed into the narrow hull, where one of them is waving for help. Next to the boat, a sailor is floating in the sea. Standing on the water, Jesus is holding his hand.

Rescue.

Olek sits down in the first pew.

He studies the picture.

Black Rasta braids floating in the water.

He is seized by homesickness, like a sharp pain. Homesickness for the Virgin of Odessa, protectress of all sailors.

I'm coming to fight at your side, my love.

Protect me, too.

And forgive me my trespasses.

Amen.

PORTMÁN | SPAIN

Marwan Fakhouri

Sand.

Salty water.

His head aches unbearably, while a storm rages in his head.

He wants to lie down.

To sink into the sand.

He doesn't sink.

Strong arms grab him left and right and carry him.

His legs are like jelly.

Dry sand.

Beneath him, black sand.

Above him, black sky.

The sun, the colors—both have abandoned Marwan.

I couldn't decide. I couldn't sleep. I couldn't think of anything else anymore: Should I go or should I stay?

It was only later, in Cairo, that I realized: if you're in a war, you cannot give up. That is the end. I gave up, but it was my decision.

One more chance, please.

Back.

Back to last night again. Can you hear me, friends? I would like to say one more thing to you:

Don't make the same mistake I did. Even if you're tired, even if everything you do seems pointless, you have to carry on.

You are better people than me.
Maybe there is no hope anymore.
But I tell you: our life abroad has no purpose whatsoever.
The fear remains with us forever. I promise you, it stays.
We have no future.

Hello?
Is anyone there?
I can't see anything.
It is dark.
I am cold.
I want to get up.
He feels around with his hands.
I want to go home.
To Tartus.

Suddenly, something explodes in his head.
Everything becomes really bright.
Unbearably bright.
A white surface. An image.
Not a photograph.
A computer simulation.
He laughs.
You are blind. Mother. Father.
Mother, you don't really believe that.

Dear Marwan,

I don't know where you are right now. But I am praying that you are well. And I pray that this war will soon be over and that you will return. That everything will be back to the way it was before. Look, I am sending you a picture. This is what it will look like here soon. Assad is building us a shopping mall right here in Tartus.

Dear Mother,
   I think death is easier to bear.
   I'm sorry.

PORTMÁN | SPAIN

Karim Yacine

"Where are we, brother?"

How should he know? He has brought them to land.

The five from the fishing village disappeared immediately. It's every man for himself here.

What do you still want? Karim feels indignation rise within him. We are much too conspicuous here. There are too many of us.

He makes a random grab for Abdelmjid, the red cloth; the others follow willingly. "This way, come this way." Up against the fence.

"Where are we, brother?"

"What's this place called?"

He has no idea.

The GPS. Go on, do it.

"Portmán."

Bigger. I need a bigger overview.

He turns around, trying to orient himself.

North is that way.

There is a street over there, running along the shoreline. He points to the right. "Alicante is located that way. Go that way." It can't be far. From there, they should call someone. Their brothers. Their families. "You'll need to go separately. It's too dangerous to stick together."

General hesitation. Nobody wants to go it alone.

"Come on, get going! May Allah protect you."

The two boys are the first to vanish.

He worries about the cousin, who is still listless, sitting on the fence with his head between his knees. Karim cautiously shakes him by the shoulder. "Do it for your brother. Pull yourself together, man!"

The teacher whispers, "I'll take him with me. And what will happen to you and the..."

Karim shakes his head. Don't speak. "Just go."

The teacher pulls the cousin to his feet. "Help me, Abdelmjid."

Abdelmjid pauses and looks at Karim. "Brother."

What now?

"What will you do now, brother?"

Karim is on edge. "I'll call the ambulance, of course," he hisses. "And then I'll disappear." He gives his friend a shove. "God protect you."

They finally vanish.

Karim sits next to the injured man. He touches his chest and feels its rapid rise and fall.

"Hold on. I'll get help."

He looks at his cell phone.

Just real fast. Zohra. It rings, but she doesn't pick up.

Karim dials the Spanish emergency number.

"SOS. *Playa*. Portmán. *Rápido! Rápido!*"

It will have to do, since he doesn't know any more Spanish. They know these kinds of calls around here. He stands up.

"Good luck, my friend." He sets his phone down by the injured man, after activating the flashlight app. It will last awhile.

He walks away.

A horrible sound. He's not breathing right.

What if they don't find him?

He turns around.

Oh, *merde*.

He kneels down. "How are you doing?"

He touches his chest again.

Oh no.

Stillness.

He picks up his phone and holds it in front of the other man's face.

"Come on, please."

No breathing.

"You can't just die here!"

Not now! Karim suddenly feels panicked.

He can't hear any sirens.

Nothing.

It is entirely still.

The moon emerges from behind a cloud.

Everything grows bright.

Only the beach remains black.

Death.

Karim carefully searches the dead man's pockets for something, some kind of identification. Who will miss you? You're a son. Brother. Husband.

He finds a couple of dollar bills in the pants pockets. A passport.

He holds it up close to his phone.

Syrian.

A Syrian passport.

A Syrian passport is worth money.

Deportation ban.

Asylum.

A future.

A future with Zohra in France.

He flips through it hastily.

The photo. They all think we look alike anyway. He is a couple of years younger. Other than that, it should work.

Karim's heart pounds.
A new identity.
What's your name?
What's my name?
"Marwan."
Marwan Fakhouri.
"My name is Marwan Fakhouri."
I'm a Christian.
A new beginning.

Lalita Masarangi

She has no idea what time it is.

How long has she been standing here?

At the bow.

Alone.

She is so angry.

She took Mrs. Malinowski back to her cabin and called her dad. She has a company phone for emergencies.

"Dad. What can I do? I can't stand it anymore."

She told him everything.

We lost a crew member.

Someone was taken off the ship secretly.

Something is not right here.

"Do something." *Dad.*

Her father listened and said nothing. She began to think the line had gone dead. No, she could hear him breathing.

"Listen, daughter. I had a call from Miami yesterday. Questions. People are not happy with our staff."

One more report like that, her dad said, and they will start hiring the Israelis again. They won't be at war forever.

"No. Daughter, now listen to me. Gold Cruises is our biggest client."

No back talk.

Hung up.

Didn't give a shit about Jo.

No one gives a shit.

She wants to scream.

She screams.

Into the wind. Into the night.

Until there are no more screams left.

The *Spirit of Europe* glides across the sea. She sees them suddenly in the moonlight.

The dolphins.

She turns around, but there is no one else to see them.

Their bodies, arcing high out of the water, gleam in the moonlight. They are playing.

Lalita turns away. She presses the button for the sliding door.

Promenade deck.

The Dolphins at Dawn are playing, but no one is there to listen.

It must be late already. Empty shopping malls. Sad.

Her whole life is an abandoned mall.

In Aldershot. Here. Everywhere.

Slowly, she walks toward the stage.

The musicians are wearing chunky designer watches.

Raymond is singing. He sees her coming and turns toward the others. The music stops.

You are just assholes, too.

She keeps on walking.

Behind her: "'Anak.' 'The Lost Son.' For Jo."

Fuck you, Jo!

AUTHOR'S NOTE

The novel *Collision* is a fictional account of a raft and a cruise ship crossing paths in the Mediterranean. This work of fiction was based on documentary research. We made a film about the real scenario, which was premiered at the Berlin International Film Festival in 2016. This enabled me to develop characters from an actual situation. They do not exist, but they could have. The plot also never happened, but it perhaps could. I will leave that to the readers.

Merle Kröger, September 13, 2017

ACKNOWLEDGEMENTS

I would like to thank those who accompanied me during my work on *Collision*:

Philip Scheffner for his ideas, criticism, patience, and much more.

Meike Martens, Tina Ellerkamp, and Rubaica Jaliwala for their feedback and support. Ilonka Brill and Robert Fischer for our joint research trips to Spain. Houari Bouchenak Khelladi for the research in Algeria. The pong film team: Bernd Meiners, Pascal Capitolin, Volker Zeigermann, and Caro Kirberg. Alexandra Gerbaulet for her assistance with the photographic research.

Terry and Sean Diamond for long drives and countless stories about Belfast and Donegal. Abdallah and Rhim between Algeria and France. Captain Leonid Savin and the crew of the *Smaragd* (which obviously would *not* keep traveling) for their hospitality and an incomparable 24 hours on the Mediterranean. Also, the team at MarConsult Ship Lines in Hamburg, and the entire team at Salvamento Marítimo in Cartagena, particularly Miguel Belmonte-Nieto, Nicolá Campoy Pomares, and Pedro Paredes Carrasco. Sigrid Scheffner for her powerful description of Parkinson's. The Abou Naddara film collective (vimeo.com/user6924378/videos) for their film documentation of the war. Lee Robin Hornbogen for his first-class fitness coaching. Britta Lange for graciously sharing with me her research on the Half Moon Camp in Wünsdorf. Anita Müller for her films and connection with Odessa. Oliver Bottini for his tips about Algeria. The crew members and anonymous passengers on one of the largest cruise ships in the world. The Blue Waters Band for "Anak" on an empty promenade deck, as well as Eui-Ok Shu, Susanne Herbeck and Anke Mueller-Eckhardt for their support.

The Scheffner, Harten, Heuck, and Kröger families in Berlin, Hamburg and Schleswig-Holstein. My friends, especially Jörg Heitmann, Susanne Schultz and Dorothee Wenner. My colleagues at pong film, as well as the team and participants in the Professional Media Master Class at Halle (Saale).

The publishers and editors Else Lauden and Iris Konopik, and the entire team at Argument Publishing in Hamburg, as well as the HERLAND network of feminist crime writers in Germany.

For the English translation, I would like to thank my US publishers at Unnamed Press, especially Chris Heiser, the translators Rachel Hildebrandt and Alexandra Roesch, and the Goethe Institute. You all took great efforts to bring this book into the English speaking world.

SOURCES

"Anak": Music and lyrics © Freddie Aguilar, 1978

"Did you Close the Door Softly?": Poem © Ruth Lansley, nee Kormes

"Wünsdorf, Halbmondlager": Audio recording PK 307-01 and PK 308-01, Lautarchiv at Humboldt University Berlin, translation from the English (Rubaica Jaliwala / Santanu Das) into German by Britta Lange / Philip Scheffner, © Jasbahadur Rai, 1916

"Bullet with Butterfly Wings": Lyrics © Billy Corgan, Music © The Smashing Pumpkins, 1995

BIOGRAPHIES

Merle Kröger is co-author and producer of the award-winning cinema documentaries *Day of the Sparrow* (2010) and *Revision* (2012). Kröger has published several novels and was awarded the German Crime Novel Award 2013. She will be releasing a documentary film in Germany based on the events that served as the inspiration for *Collision*, a bestseller in Germany. The film, entitled *Havarie*, is available in the US through the Goethe-Institut.

Literary translator and founder of Weyward Sisters Publishing, **Rachel Hildebrandt** has published both fiction and nonfiction works in translation, including *Staying Human* by Katharina Stegelmann (Skyhorse) and *Herr Faustini Takes a Trip* by Wolfgang Hermann (KBR Media). Her recent translations include *Link and Lerke* by Bernd Schuchter, *Fade to Black* by Zoë Beck and *Collision* by Merle Kröger. She is the founder of the Global Literature in Libraries Initiative.

Alexandra Roesch is a bilingual translator based in Frankfurt am Main. She grew up in England, studied Business and Modern Languages in London and initially worked in the Banking Industry before moving to Germany in 1997. She recently completed a M.A. in Translation at the University of Bristol, including extensive studies of Alfred Döblin, Günter Grass and Ralf Rothmann. She translates extracts and short stories for major German and Swiss publishers.

CPSIA information can be obtained
at www.ICGtesting.com
Printed in the USA
LVHW02s0409101117
555714LV00001B/1/P